the ANGEL in her

AN UNEARTHLY SINS NOVEL

Stefanie Dawn

The Angel in Her
An Unearthly Sins Novel

Stefanie Dawn

Disclaimer: The material in this book contains graphic language and sexual content and is intended for mature audiences, ages 18 and older.

ISBN: 978-1763870420

Editing and Proofing by Swish Design & Editing
Book Design by Swish Design & Editing
Cover Design by Opium House Creatives
Published by Angels and Fire Books
Cover Image Copyright 2022

DEDICATION

For Ashleigh, Kathy, Sue, Jourdan, and Bella.
Beta readers happy to share my darkness, first
draft errors, and all.

the ANGEL *in her*

AN UNEARTHLY SINS NOVEL

PROLOGUE

Her name is Evie, and believe me, the connotations of that name aren't lost on me.

I saw her naked once before we met.

I didn't mean to. I was simply trying to check on her as I had with many others in the city. Knowing the danger they put themselves in to steer clear of that one final step to homelessness, I checked on as many humans as I could as often as I could, and when I was able to, lead them to the pathway of a better life.

When they would let me.

I had no way of knowing I'd find Evie like that.

Of course, I should've suspected there'd be a high chance of it, given her job as a sex worker and the building she was in—that seedy hotel they use to conduct business. But still, she caught me by surprise. She couldn't see me, it was too dark outside, and internally, it eats me up to admit I watched her longer than I should have.

I should've turned away the moment I realized I had caught her at a vulnerable moment, or at least closed my eyes and waited until she was decent and dressed.

Her fare had just left. Other areas have different names for them—customers, tricks. But here, they called them fares, and while there was the rare one who simply sought some company, the sex being incidental, most of them were the scum of the city. Those who lived other lives elsewhere and came here to take out whatever sick desires they had on those who had no choice once you showed their handler the cash.

Before he left, he had hit her, and I knew it wouldn't have been the first time he had laid hands on her like that.

I wanted to go to her then and there, but swooping in through the window of a fifth-floor room while she was naked and vulnerable was a terrible idea. I had the control in me not to do that.

Barely.

But I didn't have the control not to follow that man as he left her room, nor to stop myself using fear to remind him what would happen if he ever struck a woman again.

I should've walked away and been saved from the pain of having to leave her.

There are a lot of things I should have done differently.

When I went back to check on her, instead of leaving as soon as I saw she was okay—as okay as she could be at that moment—I watched her for a while. She wasn't the first woman I had seen naked, of course, but her body told a story. The way she moved spoke of grace. Perhaps when she was younger, she was a dancer. Yet her eyes told me any confidence she had wasn't in who she was as a person but merely in her outward appearance. Her curves spoke of someone who took pride in her body, even if she felt she had to keep it that way for the job alone. Blonde hair cascaded down her back and made me think of what the fares would see in her. They'd visualize whatever remaining innocence she had and how they longed to take it from her, to break her, to shatter whatever life and light she had in her eyes, so they could feel as though they owned her. Perhaps that would make them feel better for their petty existence.

It made my blood boil.

But her scars told a much different story.

I didn't scar, but if I were scarred from emotional distress, my body would be a tapestry of all the horrors I had seen and all those I hadn't been able to save.

Perhaps that's what pulled me to her.

Her scars spoke of a woman who had been

through abuse and of a woman who at least once had enough of the pain and tried to take it away herself to flee from this world.

The scars made me want to care for her, but everything else made me want to take her.

Not only away from this city and lifestyle, but away from everything and to be with only me.

It made me long to *take* her in a way I shouldn't think about.

Her skin looked soft. I longed to touch it and do much more.

These were dangerous thoughts to have for a man who was supposed to be rescuing her, showing her a better life, and caring for her as a lost lamb.

These thoughts were even more dangerous for an angel to have.

I am Zaqiel, and if I am to fall, it will be because of her.

CHAPTER
1

ZAQIEL

You know your life is messed up when a demon has to save you.

A *demon* for God's sake.

I looked at the sky apologetically after the thought slipped through my mind. Being on Earth, with these humans, was making me lax, changing me. I had already sinned too many times, and it was more than I'd have ever thought myself capable of while in the Silver City.

Evie had been in trouble, and I got there too late.

It ate me up inside. Every moment now, it's all I could think about. I was a Watcher and supposed to be here to protect. It didn't matter I was watching over someone else at the time because when Evie needed me, I wasn't there.

He was, though.

I had watched as he had mutilated that man in front of her with rage burning through my veins. Sure, he told her to close her eyes, and I saw her huddled up in the corner of the alleyway with her eyes squeezed shut and hands clamped over her ears, whimpering. He took his revenge on the man who had tried to rape her, and I should've been angrier than I was at the way he handled it.

But part of me was glad he had found her before me because I couldn't have taken such violent action, not like that.

But demons didn't have the same rules we did.

Frank had been on Earth for some time now and had made quite a name for himself as the CEO of an architecture firm. What he was doing at this end of the city, this far from his penthouse apartment and office building, I didn't think I wanted to know. But he had saved her and even walked her home.

I followed, keeping to the rooftops.

When she had invited him into her home as a thank you, I gritted my teeth against the urge to scream at her not to let him in. She didn't know what he was, and while I knew he wouldn't hurt her, I didn't want him to sleep with her either. She was responding to that inner part of him, those alluring powers of evil that never ceased to amaze me. The darkness seduced a lot of people—it wasn't her fault.

He turned her down, and I breathed a heavy sigh

of relief. Although I had hoped she wouldn't have really done it, maybe she'd have remembered me and stopped herself in time, and his spell over her would've been broken.

Maybe I was kidding myself.

Waiting until Frank was down the street and Evie had closed her front door, I flew down and landed in front of him. He wasn't surprised to see me. He knew I had been watching.

"Careful, Zaqiel, someone might see those pretty gray wings of yours." Frank smirked as I folded my wings away, and they disappeared against my back. He was right, it was foolish to fly where humans could see my wings. But any human looking out their window wouldn't have seen anything before I folded them against my back, rendering them invisible. It was too dark outside.

I hoped.

The truth was, I was too angry to think it through, and the realization of my error only served to increase my anger.

"I had her, Frank."

He smirked again, the look that made my rage boil further. He knew how angry he was making me. "Yeah, I could tell by the way that guy was ripping her stockings off."

I stuttered. I couldn't even find the words to retaliate. He didn't know that I *almost had her.*

Only days ago, she'd have given herself to me.

And I'm the idiot who let her go.

Frank laughed, loud and booming. An obnoxious laugh from an obnoxious man.

Demon, not man. *Demon.*

"Don't worry about it. I took care of it," he crooned.

"I don't like how you *took care of it.*" I sneered at him, knowing full well the culprit was still lying in that alley in a puddle of his own blood.

He'd live.

I was angry, but I wasn't stupid. I wasn't going to help her attacker—he could find his own way to a hospital. Although I can't imagine how he'd explain to the doctors what had happened, what he had been doing that had led him to be injured like that.

As though reading my thoughts through my sneer, Frank smiled again, an easy, lazy smile that spoke of arrogance. "I took care of it in a way you couldn't," he growled. "*Permanently.*"

He was right, the man was unlikely to rape again. I doubt he'd even go near a woman again after what Frank did to him. It wasn't a punishment I'd have done, of course, but part of me had to admire Frank's creativity.

Giving the rapist a choice between his dick and his balls and telling him he can only keep one or the other. *Genius.*

Dark as hell but genius.

"Just stay away from her," I said with as much

command as I could summon.

Frank chuckled again, closing the gap between us with a few large strides. I was tall, but he still looked down on me, built like a tank.

"Don't you want to know how her lips tasted? How wet she got when I stood close to her?"

The rage flared inside me until it felt like a balloon had burst. I didn't see red, I saw white—a blinding white flash as it crossed over my vision—and I knew it had changed the colors of my eyes as the strength that lingered within me rose to the surface.

"You wouldn't." I gritted my teeth against the rise of rage that threatened to tip me over the edge.

"You're so sure of that, huh? Why didn't you swoop in and stop me? Be her knight in feathered armor?"

"Because I knew you wouldn't touch her, and she wouldn't have slept with you."

"Sure, she wouldn't." Frank was laughing again. "I won't go near her again, but you better be sure you're there if she needs you."

He purposefully stepped around me as I stubbornly stayed still, turning only when I heard his footsteps fade. As I watched him retreat, he turned and saluted me, laughing again, before disappearing into the darkness.

Where he belonged.

As the horizon cleared, preparing for an eventual sunrise, I stood, carefully unfurling my wings and shaking out the stiffness from a long night. I squinted into the distance but knew the sun's beauty would be lost on me this coming morning. When I first came to Earth as a Watcher, a helper, I'd watch the sunrise every morning. Basking in its multi-colored glow, I marveled the people here could experience this miracle every single day and not be blown away by the magic of it.

But I understood now.

The people—they were sullied—the purity and integrity of humanity had been tainted long ago. I, along with my brothers and sisters, had witnessed this decline until we had enough and decided something needed to be done. One by one, we came to Earth until some of us started falling, dragged down to the level of humanity by giving in to their desires, not putting their duties and faith first as they should.

This world, though, it could drag the light out of almost anyone. There was a lot of darkness.

Especially in cities like this one.

One end of the city would be dazzling riches,

high-rise offices, and apartment buildings that screamed luxury and money—a world for the elite, for those who were willing to claw their way to the top by stepping on those down below.

Not all of them, of course. I'm sure there were many good people at the other end of the city. I couldn't know for sure, though, as I never saw them.

How many do you think came here to help those who needed it most?

It's no wonder this city attracted such a large demon population. They could party and do whatever they wanted, surrounded by the cream of society, and then if they still fancied it, come to this end of the city and find the darkest, dirtiest streets and alleys to fight and really let go of the demon inside them they couldn't completely contain.

Not as well as they thought they could anyway.

The contrast from one end of the city to the other was depressing at best and downright degrading at worst. It's no wonder the people here had lost that spark, that light in their eyes and hearts that displayed the faith they still held. For what did they have to show for any faith they had left? They had been cast aside by society and left to fend for themselves, scraping together what they could of what had been left by those who already had too much.

We couldn't save them all, but we couldn't simply leave them to live like this either.

Sitting on the roof's edge, I dangled my legs over the side and stared hard at the front door to Evie's apartment building. I didn't expect her to come back out after Frank had walked her home, but I stared anyway, just in case she was foolish enough to do something stupid. She'd had a rough night, as she often did, but tonight was harder for Evie than the others. She had been attacked, almost raped, and I dared to be thankful for Frank's intervention.

The *one* night I had torn myself away from her. The first time in *days* I hadn't been watching her. The *one* night I told myself no matter what happened between us, I was here to help others too and couldn't be devoting all my time to the one person.

That was the night she had been attacked.

Of course.

What was it people said? *Murphy's Law.*

Well, Murphy can burn in...

I sighed.

When she really needed me, I wasn't there. Obviously, I tried to help as many humans as I could, but the things that drew me to her in the first place were still heavy in my chest, and I couldn't get away. Part of the problem was I didn't think I *wanted* to get away. If I couldn't keep her close, I wanted her in my mind.

What drew me to her in the first place?

I imagine the oldest story in the book—a

prostitute with a heart of gold.

But she didn't only have a heart of gold. She had a spirit of fire, a fire that burned so bright it threatened to consume us both when I got too close.

And I very nearly did get too close.

Maybe it was because, before her, there were so many things I had never considered. She made me see humanity, or more specifically, her, in a way I hadn't seen women before. She represented freedom and desire. However, she'd tell you freedom was a prison of its own and came with consequences, but that's because the type of freedom she lived wasn't real. I could give her real freedom.

I shouldn't want to. I shouldn't see her the way I did, but she filled up the recesses of my mind. Evie was a permanent fixture now, as part of me as I was a part of this city.

Maybe when it came to her, I was no better than human.

She's too good for a life like this. More than once, I know she had taken on clients she knew to be violent to save the younger girls, girls who were too young to be on the streets in the first place. And like Evie, I had devoted much of my time to saving them, getting them off the streets, finding them places to live and jobs, so they could make a new start.

Sometimes I wish I were more like Frank, so I could seek my revenge on the abusive partners or neglectful parents who had pushed these young men and women into a position where they felt taking to the streets was their only option. The irony, an angel wishing he was more like a demon.

But that wasn't the right way to help them, and I still had enough faith within me to do it the right way. Because if angels were like demons, well, then we'd all be in trouble.

She wasn't the only one, was she? Evie wasn't the only escort who also had a kind heart. A lot of them did. Many were pushed into this life through no fault of their own. They were out of options, had no one to turn to, and would fall into the path of someone who had no qualms about taking advantage of them.

No, she was different because she almost broke me.

I couldn't wait any longer.

Despite my previous broken promises to myself that I'd stop watching her like this, I stood and walked along the ledge until I was level with her apartment near the back of the building and sat again.

An hour dragged by slowly, and I made sure to keep my wings folded up so they couldn't be seen by prying human eyes despite how good the night air felt on them. Keeping them folded all the time didn't feel nice. It was like wearing a sack over your head, unable to breathe or see right, counting the seconds until it would be lifted, and you could take that first breath of fresh air and feel the sun on you.

It was a sad truth of this area that if they saw a random man wandering the rooftop, they wouldn't think anything of it.

But wings—they would draw attention and raise many unwanted questions.

Watching her, she crossed the room to have a shower after crying for some time.

I wished she'd keep her curtains closed.

She returned to the bed, sitting on the edge of the thin mattress with only a flimsy towel wrapped around her, stretching her arms to the ceiling as though in a silent hallelujah that she had made it through another night.

I wanted to touch her again, to run my fingertips under that towel…

I scolded myself.

I'd *not* become one of the fallen.

Another lie I told myself as Evie stood and walked out of my line of sight.

I couldn't take it anymore.

Unfolding my wings, I swooped.

CHAPTER 2

EVIE

Three Weeks Earlier

Dipping the cotton wool back in the antiseptic solution, Heidi hissed as I dabbed it against the cut above her brow. Her knuckles turned white as she gripped the mattress where she sat. It was a deep cut, and she should probably get stitches. But I supposed I should be thankful she was letting me clean her up and treat the wound as there was no way in hell she was going to go to a hospital.

I'd scold her for it, but I would have done the same.

And had on many occasions.

Hospitals asked too many questions. They wanted to make police reports, then those men in blue would simply stand at the end of your hospital bed and smirk as if to say *you're a prostitute, you brought it on yourself.*

I preferred the term escort myself, but who was I kidding?

"Sweetie, you can't see that man again." I hummed as I patched up the cut with a bandage, the guilt heavy in my stomach as Heidi sharply sucked air between her teeth. It was hard to cause her pain when she had been through so much, even though I was doing it in her best interests. She'd have one hell of a bruise, probably a black eye too, and if the cut didn't heal right, likely a scar across her brow as well.

She pouted, wincing when the expression stretched the split in her lip, causing a fresh drop of bright red blood to glisten from the wound. "You only call people sweetie when you're angry."

"I'm not angry at you."

"But you're angry." When I only hummed, she continued, "Paul likes blondes."

"Tyson has plenty of blondes to offer him," I answered.

Including me.

Tyson, our *manager.* Seriously, of all the fake titles he could give himself to cover for the term *pimp,* and he went with *manager.*

Heidi turned her head, staring out the window as her lip started to tremble. "He likes the way I scream," she whispered.

Honestly, I thought I was going to vomit. Swallowing it back, I took her hand and patted it with my other one while I gritted my teeth against the rage. To hand over one of your girls to a man who was known to get violent was bad enough as it was, but to give him the same girl over and over for such a sick reason.

I swallowed heavily at the burning bile rising in my throat. The fucker probably paid extra to Tyson, who wouldn't turn down cash over a few cuts and bruises.

And broken ribs.

I didn't want Heidi to have to be here, to be doing this with her life. She was young, too young. She told everyone she was eighteen.

I wasn't so sure.

"I'll take him next time," I said.

Heidi whipped around to face me, terror in her eyes. "You can't. Tyson will know I told."

"I'll change the fare's mind, and he'll want me instead."

"I can't ask you to do that."

"You're not asking." When she opened her mouth to answer, I stood. "Heidi, shush. Shut it and let someone take care of you for once."

"Evie, there's taking care of, and then there's being stupid." Her eyes were so blue, I could see why the fares liked her. Heidi radiated innocence. So, as she stared at me with those bright eyes, shining with tears, I knew I needed to do what I had to do to protect her. I could handle the fare.

I'd had worse.

I shushed her gently when she went to protest again, but I could see exhaustion was taking hold of her. Her eyelids were drooping as I lay her down, and her breathing had steadied before I had finished tucking her in. Brushing her hair away from her face, I sighed. This was no life for her.

If I couldn't get her out of here, the least I could do was protect her. She was afraid of Tyson, but I wasn't.

Liar.

Okay, that was a lie. I was afraid of him. I'd be stupid not to be. But I found if you don't show fear, he's less likely to beat you.

I had brought Heidi back to my apartment after I found her slumped against a wall on a street corner, bleeding and crying with a handful of cash clutched in her fist. I had to see Tyson. Once in the hall, I locked my front door from the outside. She wouldn't be waking any time soon. It was almost four in the morning as I made my way out onto the street to find Tyson. He wouldn't be hard to find, he was always at the same bar. I only hoped he wasn't surrounded by too many of his friends. He tended to get cocky then and was more likely to do something stupid to show off to them.

The worse part about it was Tyson was the lesser

of evils. He may beat us occasionally, but he provided rooms in a run-down local hotel to sell ourselves, away from our apartments so we never brought the fares home. He rarely skimped on our cut, although he did control our rent and spending money, and he protected us from the gangs who roamed the streets.

I knew it was off to consider his control and occasionally violent treatment to be the best option, but I knew better than most the evils that lurked in the world.

So I guess if I had to be living in this shithole of a city, on the wrong side of the tracks, I might as well be protected from the worst scum of the Earth by a slightly less scummy jerk.

I found Tyson at the Union, his regular bar.

Of course, where else would any self-respecting pimp be at this hour?

The bar was across the street from the hotel where we worked, so it made sense. He could watch the girls come and go.

But that also meant he'd have seen Heidi as she stumbled toward my place.

I stomped my way into the bar, wishing I had made a quieter entrance when I realized Tyson was surrounded by eight of his friends.

Fuck.

"Evie," he exclaimed as I approached with much more tentative steps than when I had entered, and he scooped me close to him with a large arm and squeezed my ass through my skirt. His friends laughed appreciatively, already standing from their stools and moving around me, so I was surrounded, all before I even had a chance to say anything. Intimidation, the first tool of a pimp. "To what do I owe the pleasure?"

"Tyson—" I started.

"Evie," he slurred. He was drunk. Great. "How long have we known each other?"

"Too long," I muttered. I'd lived at this end of the city my entire life and been bouncing between houses for years before the apartment I could afford only under Tyson's employment because he controlled it. While it wasn't great, it was the first permanent residence I had occupied in almost a decade. The first place I could almost call my own. "Six months," I answered after his expression darkened.

Apparently, he wasn't in the mood for my attitude.

As if he ever was.

"You know, I've never slept with any of my girls," he drawled.

"Good for you. Listen, we need to talk about Mr. Gilbert."

"Ah, yes, Mr. Gilbert, a very high-paying customer." Tyson chuckled, patting his pocket while his team of cheerleaders laughed again. He still had his arm around me, and it was uncomfortable. The difference between his physical stature and mine wasn't lost on me, and while he wasn't particularly tall, he was built and could hurt me easily.

I should know.

"I'm taking him next time he comes to you," I said.

"He likes Heidi."

"He can't have Heidi anymore."

Tyson's brow furrowed as he watched me through the alcohol daze as his entourage closed in around me further. "That's not up to you, Evie," he whispered.

I tried to repress the shudder that ran up my spine. "He'll like me, I promise," I said, and when Tyson looked at me skeptically, I leaned in close to his ear and whispered, "*I can scream.*"

His eyes widened, and I felt sick again but kept my expression neutral as he surveyed me.

"Heidi needs to learn to keep her mouth shut," he muttered, then said nothing more. I didn't like it when he was quiet. There was something so much more menacing about a whispered threat than a shouted one.

I placed a hand on his arm and fluttered my eyelashes at him. "I *made* her tell me. You know how persistent I can be."

I held my breath until he chuckled. With any luck,

he wouldn't remember the full details of this exchange tomorrow, only the outcome. When he grinned at me, I knew I was out of the danger zone, and my shoulders drooped slightly as I relaxed.

"Yes." He sucked his tongue against his teeth, making a few clicking sounds as he ran over the thoughts in his mind. "I know what a pain in the ass you can be." His eyes flickered over my shoulder, and I realized it too late.

There'd be a price to pay for asking Tyson for something.

There always was.

A hand clamped over my mouth before I could scream, and a large armed wrapped around my torso, pinning my arms to my sides as I stared at Tyson, pleading with him, wide-eyed. There was no sense in pretending I wasn't afraid. I don't think I had it in me anymore to cover the fear. I was always so carefully holding myself together around him, and I had allowed myself to relax, foolishly thinking our conversation had ended.

I blinked my way through the tears that threatened to surface and stared at Tyson as he smiled.

"Since I'm doing you a favor, you can do one for me." His eyes flickered again to the man standing behind me. I knew nothing about him except his physical strength and barrel-like chest I was pressed against. "And Kenrick here has been looking at getting into the business, so maybe you can show him how a good whore fucks."

My scream of *no* was lost against Kenrick's hand as he dragged me backward through the bar.

CHAPTER
3

ZAQIEL

"I can't help you unless you *let me* help you."

It seemed I had said those words a lot since being in this city. Other places, other times, and people were more open to help. But here, the distrust of strangers, and even families, ran thick through the residents' veins. They figured if I was offering them help, then I must be doing it to gain something from them, and usually, the price was too high to pay for whatever was offered in return. A price they were unlikely to find out until they had made a proverbial deal with the devil.

If only they knew the truth.

So, of course, they didn't believe there was nothing I wanted in return, so I had to show them. But first, that meant pestering them until they let me help. Although sometimes, even that wasn't enough, and people got violent. Sometimes I simply had to leave them be, which hurt more than seeing them in pain in the first place because it felt like they were choosing the pain out of some misguided understanding of my motives. What's really happening is they were choosing their current pain over the potential unknown pain of letting a stranger into their lives.

I understood, but that didn't make it any easier to stomach.

"I can help *you,*" she crooned, her lips close to my ear as she pawed at my chest through my clothes. Her hips were constantly in motion as she moved against me in time with the loud music in the club, like all those girls on the stages dotted around the room. I didn't look at them, I only watched her. I knew she was beautiful. I wasn't blind. The tight red dress she wore left almost nothing to the imagination, hugging around her waist and petite breasts. But I didn't see her that way. She had been openly flirtatious since I approached her, and I could tell she was looking for an escape from her reality—one night away, where she could pretend the rest of the world didn't exist.

She was lucky she ran into me, for I don't imagine many of the men here would have the same intentions I did.

But she was lost, a lamb in need of shelter and care.

She was beautiful, but I wasn't here for pleasures of the flesh.

Grabbing her shoulders, I held her at arm's length and watched as she gazed at me, heavy-lidded with her ruby red lips parted in silent invitation.

"There's a women's shelter at the edge of the city. I can take you there, and they can help you."

Her demeanor changed in an instant. "Fuck the shelter. They'll keep me for three days, then send me home."

The look of seduction vanished from her face and was instantly replaced with anger. The pout dropped, and her lips pressed together as her frown darkened her features. When she tried to pull free from my grasp, I increased my grip on her shoulders.

"You're hurting me," she whispered.

"*He* hurts you," I said.

She stopped struggling, and with wide eyes, took me in again, her gaze sweeping up and down my body as though looking for some outward sign I could be trusted or, perhaps, a large sign flashing the words *stalker—beware*. I had been watching her on and off for a while. The man she lived with beat her almost daily, and while he didn't lay a hand on her son, I can only imagine that was through her taking the beatings instead.

She shouldn't have to.

But he kept her off the street and the dancer's pole where he found her. He pays her rent and has made her believe that she needs him, that without him, she's nothing and useless and will surely die and drag her son down with her. The truth was, while dancing, financially she was doing just fine without him. He was the one who gambled the money away, not her, and who spent his and her funds on drugs instead of food and schoolbooks. She didn't need rescuing from the club, she simply needed rescuing from *him*. He'd gotten himself so far into her head she didn't believe she was capable of anything better. I'd seen this story a hundred times over—young men and women alike who had been tricked into thinking they needed someone they didn't. They were manipulated and molded to believe this person only wanted to care for and love them and needed their devotion so much their life would fall apart without them.

It wasn't always the small woman who fell for a man physically capable of hurting her. I had learned looks could be incredibly deceiving and had come across women who were just as proficient at that level of manipulation and control, both with and without the violence.

But this woman, she kept coming back to the club, chatting with the people who worked there and knew so well she could trust them. They told her to come back, begged her, told her they could protect her, and she could even sleep in the room upstairs until she found a better place.

They were right, but she wouldn't listen.

I'm not here to rescue everyone from this end of the city, as though if we could evacuate this entire area, everyone would instantly have their problems solved. It doesn't work like that, and it took me longer than I care to admit to realize places like this aren't filled with the lowest of humanity, but also those who had run into bad luck, circumstances outside of their control, or simply born into it.

No, I'm here to offer a leg up to those who need it, however small that might be.

So I'm trying to get her to listen to me, a total stranger to her. Why I think she's going to listen, I'm not sure. But here's the thing—I have to try and keep trying, and I'll try over and over again to save as many people as I can even though I know this part of the city will never change, like thousands of others like it across the globe.

This city, though, I feel like I've adopted it as my own to care for. It's become almost a personal challenge to me. There are areas where it would be easier to help, but easy isn't why I'm here.

Every failure, all the pain, everything which adds another scar to my heart is the motivation I need to try harder. Even if sometimes I can feel the darkness leaking into me like ink, spreading through me and threatening to infect me with the hopelessness that's draped over so many people.

"Annie," I whisper, and her eyes widened further, only enhancing the look of innocence and fear on her features—deep brown eyes framed by dark lashes and even darker hair that fell around her face and ended neatly on her shoulders. "Let someone help you. If not me, then your friends here."

"How do you know so much about me?" The terror was evident in the tremble in her voice, the whisper waivered into almost nothing as she finished her question. I must be frightening to her, my frame big enough to be intimidating and tall enough she had to look up at me.

"Think of me as a guardian angel," I said.

She almost laughed. The twitch of her lip vanished when I didn't smile in return.

"Please, just leave me alone."

I released her but took a half step forward, closing the gap between us so she had to crane her neck to look at my face.

"Leave him, or I'll make him leave you."

It wasn't a threat.

Not one directed at her anyway.

Annie didn't listen, and I supposed I shouldn't have been surprised.

When she got home, the man she lived with, Wade, wasn't there. She had the chance to leave after she picked up her son from her neighbor. I waited on the rooftop of the building across from hers for her to come out, flee to the club, and into the arms of people who were willing to help her.

There was still much about this place I had to learn, and not everyone here is the sort of person you might judge them to be. The people working in the bars and clubs, the dancing girls and sex workers, and even some of the men who looked after them, were as often as not, good people doing the best they could in a poor situation. I had thrown a blanket of presumption over the entire area, and there were so many holes in that vision now, it was a needlepoint of awareness. The most unassuming people could contain the darkest souls, the deepest secrets, and the sickest desires. The tattooed six foot four, ex-con bouncer at the third-largest strip club in the city actually had three children and a wife he loved and cared for with a gentle demeanor that didn't fit his physical appearance.

Yeah, I had a lot to learn.

Apparently, so did Annie because, for whatever reason, she stayed with Wade.

I tried not to judge. It was easy to look at these people and wonder why they didn't simply *do better.* But it wasn't always that simple—it was *rarely* that simple. Annie felt she had no choice. Wade had gotten into her mind so much she felt tolerating the beatings was the best situation she could hope for.

No more.

I had stood by long enough and had pushed her as hard as I could. Tonight wasn't the first night she had seen me and only the first time I had made her aware I was there. I had encouraged her neighbors to talk to her, posing as a long-lost brother who she didn't want to see anymore. I had even gone as far as leaving anonymous notes advising I knew what was going on, and I could help her leave, hoping she'd take solace in a stranger reaching out.

I couldn't do what the demons could, and I didn't want to, but perhaps I could find a halfway point to get the good work done.

When Wade got home, he saw her red lipstick. It was difficult to remove and had stained her lips. He knew Annie had been out, and she was going to pay for it. People in other apartments surely could hear what was going on, but what could they do? Interfering could mean getting hurt themselves, and the police? How long would they take to get there? They'd lock him up for the night, he'd be back on the street tomorrow, and Annie would pay for it with blood and teeth.

I watched as Annie ran from him, grabbing her

young son and locking him in a closet as he cried and screamed. She fled across the apartment and darted by the windows of the living room to hide in the bathroom. Wade followed at a relaxed pace. He knew she had nowhere to go. The combination of his fists clenched at his sides and his casual stride sent anger pulsing through my veins. He enjoyed this.

But he didn't count on me.

When I heard the door slam and knew Annie was in the bathroom, I swooped in. In one quick motion, I leaped from the roof and unfurled my wings, then crossed the street in a split second and tucked my wings around my body as I crashed through the window into their apartment.

Wade covered his face with his arms as glass went flying across the carpet. When he looked up, the insults were on the tip of his tongue. He wanted to yell at me, threatening me for the damage and breaking and entering.

But beyond the strange man he now saw standing in his home was the impressive span of my wings, dappled steel, ash, and gunmetal grays casting a shadow across the room as they almost touched the walls on either side of me. His eyes grew wide, and his jaw dropped as he tried several times to speak, too stunned to move as I crossed the room and snatched at the front of his hoodie.

"Hey, Wade," I growled. "Why don't you pick on

someone your own size?"

I tried not to think about how Frank could've come up with a better line.

Wade screamed, more high-pitched than I'm sure he'd like to acknowledge, as I yanked him from the apartment and out the window I had entered. His fingers clawed at my wrist as I hovered above the street, taking him higher than the apartment building.

Eight stories up, the chances of him surviving a fall from this height was around ten percent.

I told him as much as I sneered.

I liked those odds.

He didn't.

His hair fluttered around his face from the pulsating wind and the beat of my wings as we moved slightly up and down with every beat. I didn't release my grip on his hoodie, but that and him grasping at my arm were the only things keeping him from gravity's unforgiving embrace.

"What the fuck are you?" he cried, and I almost smiled.

Pulling him close to my face, I shook him until he dragged his eyes from the street below and looked at me. "If you so much as *touch* Annie, or anyone else, ever again..." I let my grip on his hoodie slip slightly, and he jolted down an inch before his knuckles whitened with the grip on my arm. "Do I need to tell you what will happen?"

He shook his head but apparently couldn't find anything else to say.

Funny about that.

He finally managed to release a whimpered, "Please."

I slackened my grip again, letting him jolt down another inch.

"Did you ever stop when she begged you?" I snarled. "Did you ever stop when she screamed, *please?*"

He knew the answer, as did I.

"I'll never touch her again, I swear!"

"Or anyone else. You'll never raise your hand in violence *ever again.*" When I leaned in close to his face, he tried to lean away, the futility of the motion not lost on either of us. I let my eyes go white. "Don't think I can't find you."

This time he nodded with frantic, rapid movements.

Satisfied he understood, I nodded once.

Then I let him go.

I didn't let him die, no matter how much he deserved it. That wasn't my call to make.

I knew my strengths, and I knew I was fast enough to simply dive down and grab his ankle before he fell too far.

But it was far enough for him to see his life flash before his eyes.

His hands scrambled for purchase as I lowered him to the road, still holding him by his ankle, his fingers scraping at the asphalt as soon as it was within reach, and he fought his way to his feet the moment I let him go. As he stood, I folded my wings away and crossed my arms across my chest. Wade stared wearily at me for a moment, glancing up at the sky before looking back at me as if deciding if it had really happened.

I arched an eyebrow at him, and he ran.

I watched Annie for a few more days. She waited for Wade to come back. She had called the police after his disappearance. They had taken photos of the broken window, although none of them could figure out how he had been taken from that window as the fire escape was off the bedroom, not the living room.

When Wade didn't return, she packed up her things and took her son to the club. She couldn't stay there since the apartment was in his name. She'd surely be issued with an eviction notice soon anyway, as I'm certain with his gambling, he was behind on the rent, and who knows who was after him for unpaid debts. As promised, the club let her stay in the room upstairs. I could see Annie crying as the club owner, a statuesque woman with tattooed eyebrows, embraced her.

I stopped watching her after that.

She had found her home, her sanctuary.

So, I moved on to help someone else.

CHAPTER
4

EVIE

Four days. That's how long Tyson gave me for my bruises from Kenrick to heal. They were mostly around my neck. Apparently, he was a choker.

The time was given to me to heal only because Mr. Gilbert called, and he didn't like a woman who was marked.

Irony.

Tyson made a big deal about the favor he was doing me by letting me take the fare, claiming he didn't believe I was doing this for Heidi but because I had heard what a good payer Mr. Gilbert was and wanted the extra cash. Mr. Gilbert had argued the point, demanding he be allowed to have Heidi again, and Tyson could only talk him out of it by telling him Heidi's wounds hadn't healed.

It wasn't a lie. She was still staying with me and

would wince every time she stood. Apparently, her injuries were worse than they had first appeared.

I needed to get her out of here.

I met Mr. Gilbert at the hotel. I waited for him by the room door wearing slinky black lingerie and high heels. He swept past without looking at me when I held the door open for him, and only after I closed it and turned, did he bother to look into my eyes.

"I do like blondes," he said.

"I know," I answered, keeping the seduction heavy in my voice.

"Do you know what else I like?"

I decided to play it safe and lean into the innocent role he seemed to like. So when I shook my head, his eyes flashed with lust. "No, Mr. Gilbert."

"Call me Paul."

Paul, of course. An unassuming name for an unassuming man. I had only seen him in passing, leaving the hotel from across the road or walking down the street, away from his sins. I'm sure I imagined more of a Jekyll and Hyde situation than the man standing in front of me. He was undoing his cufflinks as he eyed me. His suit was expensive as I expected for what he pays Tyson. When he removed his wedding ring, I resisted rolling my eyes. Obviously, what he does in these rooms he wouldn't dare do to his wife, lest the public discovered he's a sick fuck.

Maybe I just hadn't met Hyde yet.

When he approached me, all I could think of was the way Heidi came to me, time after time, broken and bruised, and I imagined the sort of man who was capable of such things. I had to fight the bile rising in my throat when he kissed me, and I'm sure my lips were moving stiffly against his, the gentle touch of his kiss luring me into a false sense of security.

"Why so nervous?" he whispered against my lips, and when I shuddered, he wrapped my hair around his fist. He didn't pull or yank me around, but with every gentle touch, I was put more on edge about the violence I knew was coming.

"I just want to please you," I said, my voice quiet against him. He was so close, and I was trembling when he ran his hand down my body, squeezing my breasts on the way down as he traced his fingers over my stomach, snapping my garter against my skin and making me jump.

He chuckled, and I realized I wasn't as strong as I thought I was.

I'd put myself in some stupid situations before to save others, but it was always a spur-of-the-moment decision, fueled not only by my protective nature but by rage. So when the pain came, I had adrenaline running through my veins, protecting me from some of the reality of what was happening.

But this, this was different. I knew what this man

was capable of, and I had days of knowing this was coming, days to imagine the pain he'd inflict, and all that did was build it up to a nightmare in my mind.

"Do you know what I think?" He hummed as he ran his fingers along the top of my panties. "I think you have heard what I like. I think that other little blonde slut has been running her mouth off."

"No, Paul, I just—"

He slapped me across my face so hard my ears started ringing. He hadn't let go of my hair, and my scalp screamed in protest as he used my hair to maneuver my face to his. Tears stung in my eyes, and this unassuming man, well, his face told me there was the devil inside him.

I whimpered when he pulled on my hair, shrieking when he yanked so hard, I was tilted backward until I lost my footing. He still didn't let go of my hair and let me flail and struggle against his grip as I tried to get back onto my heeled feet, desperate to release the pressure against my scalp.

Wrapping my hands around his wrist as he pulled me upright, his hand still tangled in my hair, he laughed at the tears openly streaming down my face.

"Oh yes…" he snarled. "You'll do just fine."

He could see me. I knew he could.

Tyson, that fuck.

Although I could hardly see him, I was barely conscious at this point. My eyes felt like they had been reduced to slits, and I didn't need to touch my face to know it was swollen beyond recognition. Paul had dragged me out of the room when he was done. I didn't even know if we ended up having sex. By the time he got through with the first beating, I was in and out of consciousness. He'd wait for me to wake every time before continuing, though.

He liked it when I screamed.

When I couldn't walk for myself, he dragged me out of the room. I guess I should be thankful he didn't drag me by my hair, a courtesy to be dragged with his blood-splattered hands under my armpits. As soon as he exited the building, he left me on the sidewalk by the front entrance and whistled as he walked away into the darkness.

It was cold, and the night air stung against my wounds.

Tyson was at the bar on the other side of the street, and even though he stared for longer than he usually would, he didn't come out. He turned his head as though he was following Paul with his eyes.

Perhaps seeing me in this state, he'd think twice about giving one of the other girls to him.

It was a futile hope.

I suspected Paul had taken it out on me because I had the nerve to show up instead of Heidi, so perhaps he dished out additional punishment. Tyson must have realized it had never been this bad before.

Tyson must also have realized this couldn't continue. I'd be out of the cycle for a while as I healed, and that was money that wasn't coming to him.

I'd like to think he wouldn't serve Heidi to Paul on a platter anymore.

Then again, I'd also like to think Tyson might help me, given I couldn't even move enough to lift my head off my shoulder.

But did he come across the road to get me?

Yeah, right.

Minutes, I think. I believe that's as long as I lasted. It felt like hours because of the pain, but I'm sure it was only minutes. Nothing stirred in the night—no cars, no foot traffic—only the murmurs of music, chatting from the bar, and the faint moans from the rooms in the hotel behind me.

How the fuck was I going to get home?

My eyes fluttered closed, and the last thing I remembered was someone's legs in front of me and heavy military boots.

CHAPTER
5

ZAQIEL

I'd seen some terrible things in my time on Earth, but this, I wasn't prepared for.

I had made a habit of wandering around the city streets at night. It seemed that's when most people required assistance. My first few days at the other end of the city had been pointless, and it was only through asking around had I realized the people who needed help the most were unlikely to live amongst the high-rises and penthouse apartments or even the suburbs. Although I'm sure there's always someone around who could use a leg up everywhere I went, they just had different issues there—money and family concerns. But here, there were people who required real help.

This is where I was needed right now.

As a Watcher, I was supposed to simply do that—watch.

But my brothers and sisters and I had decided that was no longer enough. What good does watching do when there's so much pain and suffering? We could help, even if we only helped in small, indirect ways. If we guided the people, found places for them to go where they could get a head start, feed the hungry and house the cold, and encouraged them to help each other, we could help them.

God won't solve your problems for you, but he'll give you the tools to do it yourself.

If that made us angels tools, then so be it. I was happy to be used if it meant helping where it was needed—anything to ease the ache in my heart after watching humanity fall. Surely, helping was better than sitting back and simply watching them.

So here we were, my brothers and sisters and I, stationed at different cities around the world, moving on often, helping where we could.

But it was hard.

People were resistant to help, especially from strangers. They were stubborn and fiercely independent, and on several occasions when I had managed to get people out of a dire situation, they had simply returned to where they were.

I couldn't help those who didn't wish to be helped.

It was hard not to get angry at them.

So, walking around at night, I wasn't prepared to find a woman in such dire straits—slumped against a wall outside a seedy hotel, barely dressed, and beaten to within an inch of her life. Her eyes were swollen shut, and large, angry bruises were forming on her neck and face. What little clothing she had on wasn't buttoned or zipped up as though she had been hastily dressed. Her arms and legs were covered in a series of small, thin cuts—by a razor, I assume—and unsettling red stains were bleeding through her clothes in several places.

What was worse were the people in the bar across the street. From this distance, even in this lighting, I knew they could see her.

But for whatever reason, they left her there.

It would be a waste of my time to go into that bar and put the fear of God into the people who were doing wrong. By allowing evil to happen, they were no better than the perpetrator. What I needed to do now was find this woman somewhere safe and let her heal.

I knew the people here well enough to know the hospital was out of the question. If I took her there, she'd leave the moment she could walk, and no doubt end up more injured than she is now.

Her eyes fluttered briefly as I stood in front of her, but she was unconscious by the time I scooped her up, ignoring the pained groan that escaped her bloodied lips, even though the sound made my heart ache.

Holding her under her knees and around her shoulders, I turned when I heard a shout from across the road. I didn't need to know these men to know they didn't have this woman's best interests at heart. If they had cared, they would've come to help her. They must have been watching because the moment I picked her up, they were shouting and carrying on about it as if I were taking something that belonged to them. If they saw her in any way at all, it was as property and nothing more.

I didn't wait.

I bolted, keeping her curled against me as I ran.

The first corner I came to, I turned and took the opportunity to unfurl my wings and take off directly upward, landing on the roof and looking down at the men running into the now-empty alleyway. They looked behind every dumpster and pile of rubbish stacked up against the grimy walls. They looked everywhere, but it never occurred to them to look up. I didn't like the sounds of their angry shouting at each other, but from what I gathered, it appeared they assumed she had been taken against her will.

Good, that means they wouldn't blame her.

She moaned against my chest, and on instinct, I pulled her closer to me. This end of the city wasn't unknown for the sex workers that patrolled the streets. I could put two and two together about who she was and who the men were that chased me, but they had plenty of time to help her and had ignored her suffering.

I couldn't stand by and let that happen. Looking down, I watched her. Her breathing was shallow, the blood around her hairline congealing and drying. I'm certain she was closer to unconsciousness than she was to sleep. I can't imagine how anyone could sleep while dealing with that pain.

I'd take her back to my place.

She'd be safe there.

Her face—I knew it.

I didn't recognize her when I had taken her from the street. So severe was the beating she had endured and the resulting bruising and swelling, it made her unrecognizable, a morbid caricature of her former self. But as the days rolled on, and the swelling eased, even as the colors of the bruises deepened and spread, getting worse before they would get better, I realized I knew her.

I didn't know her name, but I had seen her

before. I couldn't remember exactly how long ago, but it couldn't have been more than a few weeks. A fare had hit her, and I had followed him and asked him nicely not to do it again.

No.

I had lost control in the moment and showed him the power behind my features, unfurled my wings, told him these women were under my protection, and promised him a fate worse than death if he ever laid a hand on one of them again.

He ran, and I hadn't seen him since.

But she, she was the woman with the scars that told a story of a woman who had seen as much, if not more, suffering than I had. While I absorbed the suffering of others into my soul, she had experienced it firsthand.

I hadn't undressed her. I didn't want to cause her pain or distress by moving her more than necessary. I had placed her on the bed and given her painkillers and some water. She had struggled against me trying to refuse the tablets and drink, whimpering and crying, but she had no strength left and eventually gave in.

After that, she slept for almost twenty-four hours, and I let her.

I kept a close eye to make sure she was healing. It was a slow process. It would be weeks before she looked herself again, and who knows which scars would be permanent. Would they add to the crisscross of marks already over her body? Pale white lines against her milky skin were telling a story I wasn't sure my heart could take as I wondered how hers did.

I'd never understand why humans did this to each other.

All the cheap apartments in the area were the same layout—lazy designing for lower-income earners. After the first day when she shuffled from the bedroom to the bathroom for the first time, I doubt she even realized it wasn't her place. She certainly didn't notice when she stumbled, her head lolling to the side. I was behind her to keep her steady while helping her to the bathroom, dutifully turning my back as she went before assisting her back into bed.

She didn't even notice I was there. Whether that was from the pain or the medication, I couldn't be sure, but either way, she felt like a lost puppy, simply willing to accept the help because she had no other choice. When she lay back in bed, her eyelids fluttered, her eyes still swollen.

"Who are you?" she whispered.

"I'm your Watcher Angel," I said. I don't know what made me tell her the truth, maybe because I knew she wouldn't remember, or maybe after so long of living in places of lies and deception, I craved the moment of pure honesty.

She made a sound. I think it was a laugh.

"Guardian angel," she croaked. "You're not doing a great job." And she passed out again.

I know what she meant and that it wasn't personal.

But it still hurt.

She was so used to everyone hurting her, the idea of someone not trying to was a joke. If anything, this made me more determined to prove her wrong.

I'd wake her every now and then with water, but she wouldn't eat. I wasn't sure if she could.

It was all I could do to keep the painkillers and her fluids up and keep her wounds clean, changing the dressings as necessary.

On the fourth day, she opened her eyes and saw me at the foot of her bed.

Her initial reaction was to scramble against the headboard away from me, wincing from the movement and bringing the sheets up to her chin. After the first few days, I had cut off what was left of her clothes and gently put her in one of my shirts with some boxers. It wasn't much, but I didn't want her to wake and find herself naked and think the worse.

Beyond that, it was taking too much of my willpower not to trace my fingers along those lines of her body, trying to read the story they told and maybe hoping I could soothe the pain away. Her brow furrowed as I had put her in fresh clothes, and her fingers stretched and clenched the air as if she were trying to grab me or perhaps fight me off.

She was a vulnerable woman in a lot of pain, and it was wrong of me to have the thoughts I did.

As she sat at the headboard with her eyes wide and fearful, I felt she was trying to cover her fear. I didn't move and hoped I wasn't intimidating to her. Tall and lean, I had hoped by wearing a loose t-shirt, my physical appearance wouldn't be a threat to her.

But, of course, I should've known she'd be frightened regardless.

"Where am I?" she whispered, her voice hoarse. She cleared her throat, followed quickly by a grimace. I sat on the edge of the bed and handed her a glass of water. She took it slowly, staring at it suspiciously before taking a tentative sip.

"You're in my home," I answered. "I found you on the street, beaten to a pulp, and have been nursing you back to health.'"

"Why?"

I tilted my head and thought, *what an odd question to ask.* "You needed help. You were injured."

"Why didn't you take me home?"

"I don't know where you live." I stared at her. "You were barely breathing. Do you seriously think I should've dropped you off at your apartment, even if I knew where it was?"

"Why not take me to the hospital?"

"I'm not new here. You would've left the second you could."

She stared hard at me. Every sentence was delivered as an accusation as though she was telling me off for something. I had to ask, "How did you get so badly hurt?"

If I thought her look was hard before, it was nothing compared to the way she glared at me now as though I had dared to utter some secret. I could understand her weariness of me, but the way she looked at me then, it was as if her injuries were my fault.

"It was me or her," she said so quietly I almost missed it.

"Look—" I started, but she was already lifting herself onto one elbow.

"Okay." She threw the sheet off her, trying to hide the wince the motion caused as I raised my eyebrows at her. "Thank you for helping me, but I need to go."

"I think you need to stay."

She glared at me. "Am I a prisoner?"

"Of course not, but you're not healed."

"I can take care of myself."

As she shuffled her way to the edge of the bed, I simply watched her. I could've moved and made her stay, forced her to lie back down, and held her there. But I could see a streak of stubbornness in her eyes that ran deep in so many humans and their absolute insistence they could do something themselves, even when deep down, they knew they couldn't.

When I stood, she stopped moving, watching me cautiously. I simply raised my eyebrows at her, and she continued to slide across the bed. When she reached the edge, the strain was visible on her face as she swung her legs over the side. She already had a thin sheen of sweat on her forehead from the effort. There was no way she'd make it to the door, let alone to her apartment.

As she stood, I was ready.

The second her back had straightened, she swayed, and in a beat, I was by her side, catching her in my arms as she collapsed. Her eyes fluttered open, and her lips parted when she saw my face so close to hers, one of my arms around her shoulder, and the other hand on her hip, steadying her against my torso.

Her smile was hollow.

"Oh, my knight in shining armor," she muttered.

"You're in no condition to leave. Why won't you let me take care of you?"

"I don't know who you are."

"Zaqiel."

"That clears that up. We're best buds now. Can I call you Zack?"

I made a face. "I'd rather you didn't."

She chuckled. "I'm Evie," she mumbled as I guided her back into bed, whatever strength that remained she had used in that small interaction. Sitting down next to her and handing her the glass of water again, I used the sheet to pat away the sweat on her face.

"I feel like hell, Zack," she whispered.

"Well, you look like heaven."

The words were past my lips before I even had time to stop myself. Evie arched a brow at me, and I stared determinedly at her forehead as I continued to pat her face with the sheet.

"That was a terrible pick-up line."

"I'm not trying to pick you up," I said.

She glanced at where we were standing a moment before. "Looks like you already did."

The corner of my mouth twitched. "Just stay and let me look after you. Okay?"

I expected her to argue again, but she must be feeling worse than she was admitting to herself. Because after a pause, she nodded and slid down against the pillows.

CHAPTER
6

EVIE

Apart from the obvious, I'm not sure why I agreed to stay.

Evidently, Zaqiel was right, and I was in no condition to leave. The rush to my head when I stood had white lights popping in the corners of my eyes, and I had passed out for a few seconds. When I opened my eyes, I was in his arms, staring into his blue eyes.

Those eyes were definitely judging me for trying to stand and leave in the first place.

I blinked a few times. They weren't the bright blue you always hear described, *the man with impossibly blue eyes*. No, they were a deep blue as though the depths of the oceans were beneath those irises, flecked with gray. His face was like a sculpted piece of art. His hair was dark, kept in a neat, short cut as though he didn't want to have to bother looking after it too much. It wasn't black, and I'm sure if I ran my fingers through it and let the light play off it, there'd be a world of different shades of brown there.

Fuck, he was goddamn breathtaking.

But handsome men often hid terrible secrets, and although he gave me his name and helped me back into bed, I still felt a level of unease. This wasn't the sort of city where you helped someone in need you found lying on the side of the street, much less the kind of place where you took them to your own home and nursed them back to health. People didn't do those sorts of things here. Maybe at the other end of the city, where the streets weren't caked in grime, but here, it was everyone for themselves.

So, what did he have to gain by helping me?

He said I wasn't a prisoner, but how could I truly know? Until I was well enough to leave of my own accord, I'd have to accept his hospitality and hope for the best. I imagine he'd want sex in exchange for helping me at the very least and looking at his body, unsuccessfully hidden beneath that slightly baggy t-shirt, I wouldn't mind having him on top of me.

Provided he wasn't violent like Paul.

He seems like he'd be gentle and not the sort to force.

And if he wouldn't let me leave when I was able

and wanted to, well, I'd deal with that then.

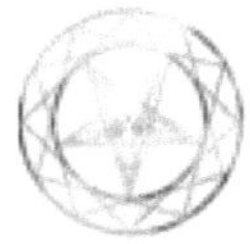

He woke me the next morning with breakfast. Sitting bolt upright when the smell of the food hit me, I immediately regretted it and clutched my head. With my eyes squeezed shut I felt the edge of the mattress depress as he sat heavily next to me, placing a palm on my cheek. Tilting my head into his touch, his palm cool against my warm skin. It felt like I had been sleeping in my own sweat for days.

Perhaps I had been.

My stomach rumbled loudly, and he almost smiled.

Almost.

It was more a twitch of his lips, a slight curving in the corner of his mouth before it dropped again. I realized I wanted to see him smile. He was a blank slate.

"You haven't eaten in days, so eat slowly."

I wanted to say *you're not the boss of me.*

But instead, I ate. Slowly.

He stayed sitting on the edge of the bed while I chewed slowly. My jaw ached with every motion, and lifting my arms too high too many times sprung up pain in my ribs. He was frowning, and I could see the pity in his eyes. I swear he was one grimace away from feeding me like a child.

I hated it—that pity.

I hated the idea of being pitied more than the idea of him rescuing me purely to get some sort of reward at the end.

I didn't need pity, I never have.

Those who pitied with that look on their face meant they saw you as below them. Something small and insignificant to be looked down upon, helped back on their pathetic feet, and patted on the head before being sent on their way. *Poor woman*, he'd be thinking, *poor little lady in this horrible situation*. How sad I couldn't do any better, that I didn't know any better than this sort of existence.

I knew better days.

Not many of them.

But I'd had a few.

Before I was bounced around the foster care system, I remember being truly happy. Maybe it's all in my imagination, and I don't have those happy memories at all. But even if that's the case, then I still know what it feels like, and one day, I don't know how or when, I'll get out of here and find that happiness again.

When my muscles ached too much to move more, he fed me, and I relented and let him. He'd break off small pieces of the toast and used a fork to feed me. It was humiliating, but I was hungry.

I hated this, but I couldn't take my eyes off his face. He was so incredibly gentle, and I was finding it hard to imagine him being violent or angry. But beyond that, what was harder to believe was there was someone in this area who wanted to help simply because it was the right thing to do, and this person had found me when I needed unconditional help the most.

I was still hungry when I finished what he had served, but he was right. If I hadn't eaten in days, then it would be foolish to stuff my face now.

Zaqiel placed the dishes on the bedside table. "Would you like a bath?" he asked.

"What? Do I smell or something?"

"Yes." My jaw dropped until I saw that almost smile of his again. He was actually joking, and something flared inside me—hope that I could maybe find out more about this man. That he wasn't a completely blank slate. If I had already spent several days here and would have to spend several more, I'd at least like to know who I was dealing with.

And a sense of humor.

Well, it was a good start.

"No." He continued, "But it's been a few days, it might make you feel better, and I need to change the dressings on your wounds anyway."

I glanced at the bathroom door. "I don't think I

can make it."

"I know you can't. I'll take you."

"Naked?"

This time it was more of a smirk. "I can put you in fully clothed if you'd prefer?"

I sighed. "I suppose you've already seen me naked." His eyebrows shot up, and I fanned the shirt I was wearing around my body, and his expression changed.

"I tried not to look." When I opened my mouth to respond, he placed a finger against my lips. Apparently, the move caught him by surprise as much as it did me, and he withdrew his hand as though he had been shocked. "Listen, I look after people all the time. It's what I do. I'll not take advantage of you... ever, and if you're uncomfortable, I won't force you to do anything. I simply asked if you would like a bath, and if so, I'll help you. You have nothing to be embarrassed or afraid of."

I stared at him.

I would admit it was a nice speech and sounded wonderful from his soothing voice—deep and reassuring. But the truth was, I had plenty to be afraid of. Lots of things both outside and—as far as I knew—inside these walls. As for being embarrassed, I wasn't usually embarrassed by my body. I tried to keep fit and looked my best. The sort of men I entertained who would see me naked wouldn't think twice about the scars because they didn't care.

Yet, for whatever reason, this man cared and wanted to look after me. I wasn't sure I wanted him to see the scars.

Would he ask about them?

Would they repulse him?

But damn, a bath sounded amazing. I still ached all over, and I could feel the dressings sticking to my wounds. I was sweaty and uncomfortable, and soaking for a while sounded like a dream come true.

So, I had a choice.

Let this strange man see me naked—not strange because he was a stranger—I was used to that part, but because of how he treated me as though I deserved something more than the life I was living or sit here and be uncomfortable until I healed fully, however long that would take.

I looked at my hands in my lap, so I didn't need to look at his face.

"Yes, I'd like a bath. Thank you."

He was strong. I mean, I should've known just by looking at him, but the way he swept me off the bed, one arm under my legs and the other under my shoulders, was like I didn't weigh anything at all. I still clung to him as he made his way to the bathroom, although I didn't need to. At no point did I feel like I was going to fall or slip, but I wanted to. He felt good under my arms with the shifting of his shoulders as he walked.

Security wasn't something I was used to, and if I could latch on to even the illusion of security while I was here with Zaqiel, while he was whatever I needed him to be in my mind and I was whatever I was to him, then I was going to take the opportunity. I didn't escape, ever. I had no holidays, no breaks, nothing to break the bleak monotony that was my existence. Because that's all I was doing— existing and surviving, day after day. What did I have to look forward to?

So, I watched his face, traced the lines of his jaw and neck with my mind as he took the few steps needed to get from the bed to the bathroom. I could pretend those arms around me would protect me always, not just for these few days I was in his care. Maybe I'd imagine I knew who this man really was, and that he was everything I needed—a man who could take me away from here and rescue me, so we'd live happily ever after with a white picket fence and a dog.

Yeah, right.

But it was nice to pretend.

He had run the bath before collecting me from the bed, and I had watched him through the bathroom door as he checked the water temperature with his fingers and adjusted the taps as needed. Now, the clear water swirled in the bathtub that perhaps once was white but now was stained yellow with age.

I didn't care. This was possibly the most romantic thing to happen to me in my entire life.

Pathetic, huh?

Girls like me, we don't get the happily ever after—we're used and thrown away. I had accepted that long ago.

He lowered me to sit on the edge of the bath, and I didn't say a word as he stripped me of my clothes. He was so incredibly gentle, his fingers nothing more than a whisper of a touch against my skin. His eyes wandered my body, but his face remained impassive. He was exactly as he had promised—a caregiver and nothing more.

When he went to help me into the bath, his hand grazed my breast, and I shuddered.

He paused, staring at the wall in front of him, a muscle in his jaw tightening, but he said nothing. Guess he wasn't as impassive as he had claimed, but it was good to know he was only human on some level, not some divine being without emotion.

Oh my God.

His eyes widened only slightly as I, honest to

God, *moaned* when I was in the water.

It felt amazing.

There was nothing special about it—no oils or bubble bath or luxury soaps. But I don't think I can describe the feeling of the water as it enveloped me, soaking away all my aches and pains and rinsing off days of sweat and grime.

And blood and tears.

It was like being reborn.

Zaqiel washed me, and I let him. He'd lather the soap between his hands before running them up and down over my arms and back, peeling away the coverings on my wounds as he came to them and discarding them. I tried unsuccessfully not to flinch as he bathed the wounds, various cuts and scrapes, and punctured skin from when Paul continued to hit me once I was swollen and bruised. Every time I flinched, Zaqiel would pause, mumble an apology, and wait a beat for another protest before he resumed his cleaning. It needed to be done, and I don't think he could've possibly been any gentler, so I tried my best to not be a wuss.

But it was hard.

There was so much pain.

"Will they come looking for you?" he asked after a while.

I scoffed. Of course, they fucking wouldn't. Tyson wouldn't waste the man-hours on me, and he certainly wouldn't have called the police. Anything

I had that vaguely resembled a family was long gone, and they didn't know where I was three months ago, let alone that I was somewhere else now in the care of a strange man, recovering from injuries inflicted by another man.

However, if Tyson saw me walking down the street, there'd be hell to pay.

I'd have to figure that out later.

I didn't know why Zaqiel was asking.

The question would hold a certain level of foreboding if it were asked by anyone else. But I figured he was asking out of genuine concern. That's what I liked to tell myself anyway. It helped with the illusion of a happy family I was painting in my mind to help with the pain.

And to also trick myself into thinking someone like him could have an interest in me beyond his duty of care.

"No, they won't come looking for me."

He nodded but didn't ask any follow-up questions. Kneeling by the edge of the bathtub, he washed my back. There were no open wounds there, only a large bruise and graze from where Paul had thrown me against the edge of a desk.

As Zaqiel traced his fingers across my back, I relaxed into his touch.

Until I realized what he was doing.

My back stiffened, and I whimpered. Gritting my teeth against any further sound, I paused, hoping he hadn't heard. His ministrations had stopped, and he was looking at me with the slightest frown. It was the first expression he had shown since we entered the bathroom.

He had been tracing the lines of the scars on my back, some of the worst ones I had.

A parting gift from my last foster father.

"Please," I whispered. I hated how weak and pathetic my voice sounded. Most of the time, I could push the memories away, but I was vulnerable here. Naked, with this man caring for me and nothing sexual about his touch, only a simple show of one human caring for another in their time of need. I hadn't felt this defenseless in a long time, and I didn't like it. Swallowing against the emotion threatening to take me over, I repeated, "Please... don't."

"Who hurt you?" he whispered.

I expected to hear pity in his voice, but underneath the monotone was something bordering on rage.

The trance was broken. The fantasy world I had created so I could enjoy this moment had been shattered, and I could feel his fingers hovering just over my back, but not quite touching. Shifting my shoulders so my back was away from him, I curled my knees to my chest and stared at the tiled wall.

Who hurt me? I thought.

"Everyone," I answered.

CHAPTER 7

ZAQIEL

Everyone.

What's wrong with this world?

How did it get like this?

There had never been a day where men weren't fighting among men. We created Utopia, and they simply couldn't get along.

I finished bathing Evie in silence. She didn't look at me.

I had crossed a line, and I knew that.

Don't.

She said don't, but I couldn't help it. *Don't ask. You don't want to know.* Underneath the tough exterior—the one she built to survive in this world, in this city—there was a wounded woman, carrying scars far deeper than the ones that ran across her body. I wanted to tell her the scars were beautiful, they spoke of someone stronger than she knew, and that while they told a story of pain and suffering, they also told of resilience and fight, of a will to live, to keep going no matter what.

One of the things I admired about humanity ran deep and strong in her veins.

There were so many things I wanted to tell her—I had seen her before and had protected her once without her even knowing.

But I didn't. I couldn't.

Evie started watching me again as I redressed her wounds. They were healing but slowly. I wished I could transfer to her my ability to heal. Maybe I could, but I hadn't tried it before. However, that would raise questions I couldn't answer.

"You made a joke before," she said as I finished dressing her in fresh clothes and laid her back in bed.

My eyebrow shot up before I could keep my expression blank. "Not sure why you're so surprised. I'm not made of stone."

She beamed at me, a soft look, lips only—the expression showed those cheekbones in all their glory, even with the remaining swelling. "You've been a blank slate. You could've been made of stone." When I said nothing, Evie tilted her head. "Why don't you smile?"

Sitting on the edge of the bed, I watched her hands, folded so neatly on her lap over the blanket.

When I raised my eyes to hers, she wasn't grinning anymore, simply watching me with curiosity. I couldn't help the frown that presented itself as I watched her lips, waiting for that lift, that brightness again, wanting to be the one who brought it to her. Wanting to kiss her. A very deep thought I was trying harder with every passing hour to keep buried. She brought out the weakness in me.

"I promise you I'm not made of stone."

I don't know if she understood.

If I could smile for her, I would, and if I could find it within me to forget the darkness outside this room, only for a moment, I'd do that too. I was starting to believe if anyone could bring that out in me, it was her. But my heart was as scarred as her skin.

Everything people did to each other hurt me.

And everything she did was a sweet pain.

Leaving her with the television remote, I heard her flicking through the channels until she settled on some daytime drama and relaxed back against the pillows. I paced the apartment through the living room, making sure to keep out of her sight.

Why don't I smile?

I think a more pressing question is what do I have to smile about?

There's a lot of darkness in this world and this city. This end of the city is one of the places where the darkness is concentrated and all the worst of the worst come, and all those desperate come when they have nowhere else to go. The weak and vulnerable, those with a false sense of power and authority, all congregate here and create the fucked-up cycle that keeps this place running.

Drugs, prostitution, gambling, crime, violence.

And all the things about humanity I can't stand.

But that's why I'm here. Because these people, most of them are innocent with nowhere else to go, they deserve some light in their lives just as much as anyone else does. There's not a great deal I can do, although sometimes I'm tempted to hit Frank up for some money, tell him he needs to put something back into the community he can so conveniently forget exists while he lounges in his penthouse apartment.

So, mostly I do small things. I keep the bad people away from the good, help those out of this place when I can, and when I can't, I try to make them more comfortable. There are many here who volunteer their time and money to help those with less, and those moments ignite the flame in my chest I thought had been extinguished long ago by all the darkness.

But still, I stay.

Because for every one person I can't help, I must try harder to help ten more.

I don't smile because, as a human, this place is depressing, but as an angel, it's excruciating.

Because I feel all their suffering and pain, I feel it as though it were my own. Where I can't take the pain away, the least I can do is offer them warmth and light that only an angel can. Even if they don't understand it, they don't need to. Sometimes, people simply need to know they aren't alone.

But Evie, she's the pinnacle of everything I'm trying to fix.

An innocent pushed to this place without choice or option with nowhere else to go. Abused, used, and rejected for most, if not all, of her life. Born into the wrong place at the wrong time and suffering because of it.

She was *my* pain, *my* suffering, and sometimes it felt like I could reignite that spark within me.

If I could only save *her.*

It sounds selfish, I know. But I also blamed myself for her being in a position where she got so badly beaten in the first place. What if I had saved her after that man hit her those weeks ago? Then she'd never have been in a spot where she was in so much danger.

I was getting personally involved, which was dangerous.

Beyond all of that, she was *beautiful.*

And I mean more than just her body. I mean her eyes, her face, her soul. Evie took the beating to protect someone, and in a horrible place where that was even a necessity, it was an incredibly brave act.

Being brave isn't the absence of fear, it's being scared and doing it anyway.

And I could see it in her eyes and hear it in her voice when she failed to contain it. She was scared. I imagined she was scared all the time, living in this place. Afraid for herself and whoever it was she was protecting, fear for a future that held no hope, fear that what had happened to her would happen again.

She was resilient, she was beautiful, she was graceful and soft, and she was a tough woman in a soft body that let her down and showed her pain like a tapestry of tales. Evie was everything I admired and desired about humanity rolled into one.

Desire is something I shouldn't even consider.

And she lived here in a world full of darkness, where those with light remaining inside would see it extinguished with whatever hope they had left if they lived long enough.

And she asked why I didn't smile.

After a few hours, I went back to check on her. When I entered the room, she immediately turned off the television and faced me, hands folded on her lap the way she does, looking at me expectantly.

"What's up now, doc? Time for my meds?"

The corner of my lip twitched a response that ignited a full grin from her. I realized I hadn't seen her smile, really smile, out of laughter. I'd seen a cheeky grin like the one she was displaying now and a look of relaxed bliss when I lowered her into the bathtub. But not the beam you get when you're not only relaxed but laughing so hard your sides hurt, the tears-in-your-eyes laughter I'd witnessed so many times, although fewer times now I was at this end of the city. Although, people's ability to find light in the darkness always warmed me from the inside out.

I wondered how long it had been since she truly laughed.

Visually, I checked her over. Evie had thrown the sheets to the side and lay on the bed, propped up against the pillows. Her legs were extended gracefully and their slender lines were amplified by my boxers she was wearing, baggy on her small frame. The t-shirt also made her appear small and vulnerable. The arms and neck were too large for her, yet somehow it managed to delicately fall over her shoulders, exposing only a hint of collarbone and drape over her breasts and curves.

Which I noticed.

These are things I shouldn't have noticed.

As though reading my mind, she added, "Is it time for my physical examination, *doctor?*"

I almost laughed until I noticed the tiniest drop in her smile, a split-second falter before she recovered herself.

And I knew she was remembering the bath and how I had touched her scars.

Before she could shut herself down to me again, I thrust a glass of water at her.

She took a grateful drink, and I frowned. "If you were thirsty, you only had to ask," I said. It bothered me that she was sitting here, needing a drink while under my care and not getting one.

She shook her head as she was midway through another gulp before smacking her lips loudly and putting the glass on the bedside table. "I don't want to be a burden. You've already done so much."

"You're not a burden."

Her eyes flashed with a moment of cheekiness again, and I was flushed with awe at not only humanity but her absolute resilience. Despite everything, all the horrible things she had experienced and been through, she was still grinning, joking even.

I was in complete awe of her.

"Well, then..." Evie started. "Do you have anything stronger to drink?"

"I don't think you should be drinking alcohol."

"Why?"

I had no reason, but it just felt like something I should say. When I only stared at her, she laughed, a light sound that traveled in the air across the room and burned into me. "I can almost see your brain working to come up with an excuse."

"A reason," I countered.

"An *excuse*. Have a drink with me, Zaqiel."

Something about my name from her lips...

I turned on the spot and left the room without another word. I did have alcohol. I wasn't impervious to all earthly desires. Spirits filled my mind with a pleasant buzzing that helped block out the darkness and also helped me sleep, and while I didn't think I could get drunk if I tried, it certainly assisted to relax me after a long day of helping.

Or failing.

Her face lit up when I returned with two glasses and a bottle. I had caught that look of disappointment she was sporting before she saw me return. As if she had been *so sure* I wouldn't just leave the room and the conversation so abruptly and had been genuinely hurt when I did.

But if that's what she was thinking, she was right. I wouldn't do that. Not to her.

So, either I was much too readable, or I had been more open with her than I thought I had.

The social graces I kept mostly to a minimum, but I made extra effort with her and for her. We had been thrust past any small talk and awkwardness and straight into an intimate situation. Not physically intimate, but emotionally and spiritually, which cut much deeper.

As I sat on the edge of the bed, I balanced one glass between my knees and flicked the cap of the bottle, sending it spinning and rolling onto the floor. Pouring in a small amount, I moved to hand Evie the glass. She glanced at the abysmally small amount of liquid in the tumbler and raised her brows at me. Rolling my eyes, which caused her to laugh again, I had to pretend that laugh didn't send a tremble up my spine and an explosion of warmth in my chest, so I poured a more generous serving.

She thanked me as I handed her the glass and poured my own, leaving the open bottle at my feet by the bed.

Looking at Evie, I caught her as she finished a sip and licked the remainder of the amber liquid from her lips, grimacing only slightly.

"Yeah…" I said, taking a drink myself, "… it's not expensive, not very smooth."

"It's just fine." And she took a gulp as if to prove

it. I had no doubt she could handle her liquor, but even she had underestimated the burn that stung her throat, and her face flushed as she held back a cough and her eyes watered.

I almost smiled, and I knew she saw.

"Come sit next to me," she said.

"I am sitting next to you."

It was her turn to roll her eyes and my turn to almost smile as Evie patted the bed next to her. "No, come sit next to me." As I went to protest, she held a finger up. "It'll make me feel less like a patient in a hospital."

She tensed as I stood as though she thought I was going to crawl over her.

As if I could stand being that close, I had already had too many thoughts I shouldn't.

So I walked around the bed and fell heavily onto the mattress, swinging my legs up and sitting next to her.

When she laughed, I raised my eyebrows at her. "You're so stiff." She giggled. My eyes darted to my pants in a moment of horror, and her cheeks flushed further. "I mean the way you sit."

"Sorry."

"Don't apologize, just relax. You've already seen me naked, more than once, so I think we can just talk."

"I'm sorry they hurt you." I felt her stiffen next to me and felt bad at having said it at all, but I couldn't help it. It needed to be said because I was sorry I wasn't there to stop it and save her. "Did you think..." I continued, "Did you think *I* was going to hurt you?"

She hesitated, and I already knew the answer.

"Yes." She took another sip of her drink. "I didn't have much reason to believe anything else."

Nodding, I took another drink because I didn't know what to say.

"Tell me about yourself," she said after a while.

"Umm..."

"Where did you grow up? What do you do for fun?"

"I devote my time to helping people. There isn't much time for fun."

"There should always be time for fun." She pouted.

"Do you make time for fun?"

Her smile dropped, and she watched me. "No, I guess I don't." That cheeky grin returned when she continued, "Wow, aren't we a fun couple to be around?"

"I like your company."

"Why?" She was still grinning. "We've barely spoken. I've been unconscious most of the time."

I didn't know how to explain that something about having her presence in this place I called home, however temporary and abysmal it may be, was comforting to me. Despite the darkness Evie was surrounded by, she was a light in an otherwise dank area. A beacon of hope and strength, and whether she saw it or not, it radiated from her.

"I'm not one for talking too much anyway," I said.

"Really? You've barely shut the fuck up since I came here." She gasped loudly, and I almost dropped my drink as I went to take another sip. "Good Lord," she cried. "Was that an actual smile I saw, Zaqiel?"

My lips, with a mind of their own, curved as I took another drink. "Maybe."

"God, I actually managed to make you smile."

After another few moments of silence, she reached across the bed and placed her hand on top of mine, curling her fingers around my palm.

"I don't think I've properly thanked you for rescuing me."

"You don't have to."

I raised my eyes to hers. She was looking at me so earnestly.

Her skin was so soft, I brushed my thumb across her fingers.

"I do, though. I've been in some fucked-up situations before, but I'm fully aware that I might have died that night if you didn't come along. Tyson certainly wasn't going to help."

"Tyson?"

"My..." Evie searched for the word, "... manager." She grimaced.

I knew what she meant.

"He'd have let you die?"

"Not on purpose, I don't think. But I know he could see me from the bar, so he might have come to get me eventually. Maybe he didn't realize how badly I was hurt."

"It was quite evident how badly you were hurt," I said through gritted teeth.

"Why do you care?" she asked, the casual tone from her voice gone, just above a whisper now. But I wasn't ready to get into that conversation, and I don't think I ever would be. I could tell her I looked after people and rescued and cared for them because that's what I did. But I knew from the beginning she was something more. I knew it the moment I had seen her scars and the pain in her eyes, a heart-shattering contrast to the beauty of her face.

Saying it out loud, at all, let alone to her, would make it much too real.

And make forgetting her and moving forward once she was gone from my life impossible.

So, I countered with a question. "Where do you go from here?"

I could see her mind reeling as though she hadn't considered she had to go somewhere beyond these walls once she was healed. Evie could stay. She could stay with me forever, just the two of us in this crappy apartment.

No, she had a life to live.

And I had more work to do.

But it seemed she was no more willing to have a deep conversation with me about the realities of life beyond this moment and this bed than I was, and she brushed my question off as I had done hers. I think we both knew there were answers to those questions and answers we weren't ready to talk about yet, if at all. So, we sat drinking in silence for a moment longer. She kept her hand wrapped around mine, and I kept rubbing my thumb across the top of her fingers pressed against my palm.

I topped up our glasses, and we talked about nothing in particular—music, whatever was the latest on the news, our favorite drinks and foods—small things of no consequence, and I could verbalize without feeling like a crack was opening in my chest. After a while, I could see her eyes were becoming glazed—the alcohol mixed with the drain in her weakened state had taken its toll. I had that pleasant buzzing in my head, and I knew I should end this conversation, but when I looked at her, I realized she was much closer than she was before. At some point, I had moved across next to her, and we sat side by side, arms touching and fingers still intertwined.

"I care because you're beautiful in more ways than you know," I muttered.

Evie looked at me, her eyes shifting in and out of

focus. I don't know if she heard.

"I'd like to kiss you," she whispered.

I stared at her, a tightness pulling at my chest.

How I'd love to take her up on that.

Maybe I could.

It was only a kiss, after all.

I leaned forward, stopping just short of making contact. I could smell the whiskey on her, and my mind, body, and soul were screaming conflicting messages at me, but I knew which pull was stronger.

When she closed the gap and pressed her lips to mine, a flame erupted behind my ribs, and I might as well have spent eternity burning in hellfire for the thoughts I had. For, at that moment, with her lips on mine and my hand reaching up to cup her cheek, she was more than a lost lamb, more than a human needing sanctuary and care.

She was Evie.

She was a woman.

She was beautiful.

She was *mine.*

And she was everything I should know better than to indulge in. I saw her in all the ways I shouldn't see a woman. But it was her, everything around me and in my mind screamed her name.

When she moved her tongue into my mouth, I jolted away. Brushing my thumb across her cheek before I lowered my hand to the bed, I forced a smile. "You need to rest."

She nodded, licking her lips again.

Except this time, instead of tasting the whiskey, she was tasting me.

God help me.

CHAPTER
8

ZAQIEL

Evie was tossing and turning in the bed, mumbles and moans escaping her lips. She hadn't slept during the day, and she had slept so much over the past few days, it didn't surprise me. But after a bathroom break and another small meal, she looked exhausted. Even the effort of the small movements she made today and simply keeping herself awake and alert, had sucked the strength from her. The weaker she got, the more fear I could see in her eyes. I hoped the fear wasn't of me, but perhaps born from the knowledge that weakness opens her up to being hurt, and she didn't want to be exposed.

I wanted to tell her she didn't need to worry because I was here to protect her. But what stopped me was the ever-present reminder that I couldn't always be there to do so.

I went into her bedroom, keeping my steps inaudible, and stared down at her on the bed.

When I placed a palm on her forehead, she stopped tossing and sighed, but a deep frown was etched into her brow.

"Can't you sleep?" I whispered.

She opened her eyes, almost shining with tears, and watched my silhouette as I stood over her.

"It hurts," she mumbled.

I thought it might. While the bath would've helped, it also would have increased blood flow to her wounds, reigniting the nerves and pain receptors. Also, redressing some of the wounds had also peeled away some of the skin that had begun healing, and the now re-opened wounds would be stinging as they were exposed to the antiseptic and throbbing with the sensation of the body frantically trying to heal them again.

I knew the alcohol was a bad idea. I didn't know how I was justifying this to myself, but I just knew.

I shouldn't have kissed her.

Moving away, I returned with a glass of water and some tablets, handing them to her. She slowly pulled herself in a half-sitting position, grimacing with every move.

"What are these?"

"Painkillers. Strong ones. They'll put you to sleep."

Evie watched me. I knew she couldn't see the details of my face in the darkness. I kept the curtains drawn, so only the edges were lit with the moonlight forcing its way into the room. She continued to watch me, holding the painkillers in her palm cautiously.

I sighed. "There's nothing I can say any more to convince you I'm not trying to hurt you. But if I wanted to drug you, I've had many chances before now." When she continued to stare at me, I sighed again, realizing perhaps that wasn't the best comfort for her to hear. Not taking an opportunity to hurt someone didn't make you a good guy, and as far as she knew, I was simply biding my time. It killed me to know she lived her life so on edge and cautious of everyone. I knew she had to be, but I didn't want her to be. I huffed out a heavy breath again, not a sigh of frustration but resignation. "Please, Evie, you need to sleep."

She waited a beat longer, her eyes darting around my face, perhaps searching for familiar features she couldn't see before she popped the tablets into her mouth and accepted the glass of water, taking a few tentative sips. Her eyes never left my face, which still couldn't have been more than a shadow as I helped her lay back down and tucked her in.

Clutching the blankets to her chin, she stared at me even as her eyelids began to droop. It broke me that there was fear in her eyes. She wanted the pain to go away, but she was fighting sleep now, afraid I may have poisoned her or given her something so I could take advantage of her. Sleep means more weakness, and weakness is danger.

I debated what to do.

Should I hold her hand?

Should I leave her alone?

Would that scare her more?

I settled on sitting on the edge of the bed, and hesitating for only a moment longer, I began to stroke her hair, curling the blonde locks between my fingers and brushing them out of her face before tracing the line of her jaw with my thumb.

"You're safe with me, Evie," I whispered.

The tear slid down her cheek as she fell asleep.

It destroyed me.

As I must have fallen asleep, I chastised myself for it.

What if she had woken up and seen me still there, sitting on the edge of her bed? No doubt she'd have thought the worse, and any trust I had earned from her would've been shattered.

That is, assuming I had any trust from her to begin with. Despite letting me bathe her, that could've been born more from desperation than trust. She was hard to read.

I didn't sleep much at the best of times, but exhaustion must have caught up with me if I had dozed off while still sitting. I watched her sleep for a moment, rolling the kinks from my neck. She was having a restless sleep, twitching and grabbing at the sheets that had been partially thrown off her.

My fingers brushed her collarbone as I moved to tuck her in again, and she sighed in her sleep.

When I had helped her bathe earlier, I had told her I wouldn't look, I was a caregiver, a healer, and I didn't see her like that.

Lord knows I wanted it to be the truth.

But there was fire between us whenever I touched her, burning embers that lit up my fingertips and threatened to consume me whole, stripping me of my status and bringing me crashing to Earth.

Which, for a moment, I thought I'd give it all up if I could just have one night with her. Just one night to touch and feel her freely, run my hands over her body, entice those sighs and moans from her lips, feel her under and around me.

I cursed quietly when I realized my body had responded to the thoughts, and I adjusted my legs. Although she was asleep, she couldn't see me anyway. She didn't even know I was here. She continued to twist and shift under the sheets, and as I moved to brush the hair from her face, her hand shot up and gripped my bicep.

I froze.

Evie was still asleep—the drugs had made sure of that. She needed the rest.

When I tried to pry her fingers from my arm, desperate to remove the distracting heat from my skin, she *whimpered.*

And God help me if it wasn't the most beautiful sound.

As I moved to stand, she grabbed my wrist with her other hand and yanked at me. Unprepared for the attack, I was pulled forward on top of her. I scrambled to untangle my feet from the sheets, freezing again when she moaned in her sleep as I braced myself over her body.

My breathing became rapid as her expression softened, and she gripped my arms, still pulling at me.

I found myself hoping whatever she was dreaming, it was about me.

The heat from her was unbearable, so close I found myself lowering slightly to inhale the intoxicating scent of her hair and skin. When she whimpered again and opened her legs, I almost cried out in frustration, my hips shifting to meet hers on an instinct I should have under better control.

No.

Heaving myself off the bed, I ignored her whimper, pulling her grip from me and tucking her arms under the sheets. I strode out of the bedroom and collapsed heavily onto the couch, breathing as though I had performed some massive act of physical strength.

And I suppose I had.

I couldn't see her from where I sat, my vision white and thoughts swirling too fast in my mind to catch. All I could feel was my cock, so hard it ached, creating a tent against the fabric of my pants. I leaned back against the couch and closed my eyes, willing away the thoughts but instead finding my hand drifting down my body and into my boxers. I groaned when I wrapped my hand around myself and opened my eyes, pausing to make sure I hadn't woken her with the involuntary sound. It seemed unlikely, not with those drugs, but the last thing I wanted was for her to wake and find me jerking off in the next room.

I couldn't stop it. My hips were bucking against my hand in desperation for friction as I worked my length, fingers wrapped around tight and thumb running over the head, dripping with pre-cum. I had to bite my lip against the urge to groan again as I felt the pleasure building.

Intense.

Uncontrollable.

I couldn't stop thinking about her body in a way I shouldn't.

In a way I mustn't.

With a frustrated roar that I muffled by slamming a pillow over my face, I withdrew my hand from my pants, denying myself the release and hating the ache that emanated from the denial.

This was a nightmare because all I wanted to do was to take her, to gently wake her from her sleep and press my lips to hers, to let her intoxicate me, and completely give in to the earthly desires that had tempted so many before me. I knew the human body, and I could touch and tease her in ways she's never dreamed. But it was so wrong in so many ways. That's not what I was here for. I was here to care for the people and watch out for them.

Not for my own pleasure.

Not to bond with a human like that.

Punching the arm of the couch, I heard a crunch as the wood underneath broke, and the arm shifted, leaning to the side now.

I was stronger than this and these desires.

Wasn't I?

Evie, you make me weak.

I couldn't get that close to touching her again.

CHAPTER
9

EVIE

The exact name of the medication Zaqiel gave me that helped me sleep the night before, I hadn't asked. But damn, they worked well. While I still felt tender the following morning and a bit raw, I was able to move with a little more ease as my body had been allowed the rest the pain was denying me. Sitting up in the bed, I inspected my arms and legs, not daring to lift the coverings but merely touching them tentatively. All the smaller cuts had healed, and I breathed a sigh of relief that I wouldn't be left with a zigzag of minor scars across my arms to match all the others I had collected. I couldn't speak for the larger wounds, though. Hopefully, given the medical attention they otherwise wouldn't have had, they wouldn't scar as bad as those left to heal without proper care.

Pressing my fingertips to my face, I wandered my hands over my skin. Still a bit tender but worlds away from where I was days ago. I was finally at the stage of healing where I could feel I was getting better. I was past the stage where my wounds throbbed, and I could feel every beat of my heart as the blood pumped underneath the damaged and exposed skin.

My elation at realizing my body was healing faster now was immediately crushed when it occurred to me what it meant.

Going back to Tyson.

Because where else was I going to go?

Tyson controlled the rent, and I'm almost certain the landlord was in Tyson's pocket, along with many others in the area. It seemed too much of a coincidence most of his girls lived within the same few buildings. So I'd have to move and hope wherever I chose wasn't simply another path back to him. But would he *let* me leave?

Would Tyson have dropped Paul as a client? While I'd like to think so, I knew he wouldn't. Paul paid too much money for Tyson to consider getting rid of him just because he busted my face. He'd probably tell him only to go a bit easier next time. Paul would probably blame Tyson for hiding Heidi from him, then he'd go back to being her fare, and there'd be little I could do to protect her because there was no way Tyson would let me take him as a client again.

I wondered if Heidi was still in my apartment and if she was okay.

Zaqiel had said I didn't have a phone on me when he found me, but he had found my spare apartment key sewn on the inside of my bra and put it aside before he discarded the clothes. They were torn beyond use anyway, and I wasn't sure I needed the reminder every time I put them on. I had asked him if I could use his phone to message Heidi. He said he didn't have one, and I believed him. With anyone else, that would seem strange, but something about him made the fact he didn't have a phone simply another puzzle piece that fit together to build the man I was slowly getting to know.

Maybe he had no one to call anyway.

I thought about going downstairs and seeing if the old public phone most of these buildings had in the lobby worked, but if anyone who knew me saw me, I'd be in real trouble. Plus, I'd have led them straight to Zaqiel's doorstep. While I'm sure he was quite capable of looking after himself, putting him in a position where he had to take on Tyson and his goons wasn't a risk I was willing to take. That, and if Tyson found out Heidi had been in contact with me, she'd bear the brunt of his anger while trying to find answers as to my whereabouts.

He'd be looking for me.

Not too hard, barely at all, but he'd be keeping an

eye out. News traveled fast amongst the girls, and even a whisper that Heidi had heard from me since I'd been *kidnapped* would mean big trouble for her. So, the lesser of two evils was to let myself disappear until I was ready to face the world again.

"You're awake."

I was wrenched from my thoughts as Zaqiel entered the room, his face somehow more passively blank than it had been before yesterday.

Had I done something wrong? I thought we had broken through the blank slate he presented me with. We had talked yesterday, really talked, and I hated to admit the way my chest ached when he didn't quite meet my eyes as he entered the room with breakfast. I asked him to stay and chat while I ate, but he just shook his head and left the room.

I didn't understand the change in behavior, and when I called after him, he didn't answer.

It honestly felt like my heart was breaking.

That was another scar I didn't need.

The next day passed with much the same behavior from him, and while I had managed to get him to sit and watch a movie with me, he kept his eyes glued firmly to the television and barely looked at me. The following day and I had enough of his shit. I was healed enough to move around the apartment on my own without much pain, so when I woke, and it was still dark out, I flipped off the blankets and went out into the living room. He was sleeping on the couch, his legs hanging off the edge of the too-short piece of furniture, his arms folded across his chest, and the blanket he had been using cast aside on the floor.

Kneeling next to him, I brushed my hand along his cheek. He was stunning—the line of his jaw and neck, the cut muscles of his chest and stomach. Those eyes, while closed, were still beautiful. Thick lashes and eyebrows, a slight frown creasing his brow as he slept.

I wanted to kiss him.

"You should be in bed."

I just about screamed. "You scared the shit out of me," I hissed through my teeth.

He kept his eyes closed, and his lips twitched into that almost smile. "Do you need another bath?"

But as soon as he said it, the look disappeared, and his face was a blank slate again. I felt as though it was a peek into the man who had previously been opening up to me, the one with a sense of humor, the one who cared beyond his role as a caregiver.

The one who perhaps stole glances at my body, even if he denied it.

"Why aren't you talking to me?" I asked.

He opened his eyes and rolled his head until he was facing me, his eyes raking up and down my body as I kneeled next to the couch.

"We're talking."

"No, don't give me that. You know what I mean. The other day we really talked and connected, and then the next morning, you wouldn't even look at me. I want to know why."

"Evie..."

It was a warning not to ask further questions, and I shouldn't have even asked this question. As though simply by being out of bed and here, I was pushing him too far. But his voice trailed off, and I didn't speak, waiting for him to say something else, anything. But he didn't talk. His eyes were pleading with mine as though there were a thousand things he couldn't say locked in that head of his. I wanted to get him to talk to me, but I didn't know how. I lifted my hand to brush his cheek again, and with reflexes that awed me, he snatched my wrist out of the air before I made contact. He didn't move his eyes from my face, and I'm not even sure how he saw my hand in the dim room.

Zaqiel held my gaze for a long while, his eyes darting between mine, and I could see the battle that now raged within him. He had told me he was a caregiver and nothing more. But then something had sparked between us which *made* it more, and for whatever reason, he was struggling with it now, denying himself the temptation.

The temptation I was to him.

Fuck, I've never met anyone like him in my life.

"Evie," he said it again, but this time the pain in his eyes was reflected in his voice. The word trembled on his lips, and his grip on my wrist slackened. I hesitated for only a moment longer before cupping his cheek and sighing at the way he closed his eyes and leaned into my touch.

I opened my mouth to say something, but what was there to say?

So, I kissed him, pressing my lips delicately to his. I expected him to pull away, to lean back, to move away from me in any way he could. But when his lips moved against mine, I swear I melted against him, moaning against his lips as I leaned forward, pressing my torso against the scratchy fabric of the couch, desperate to get closer to him. I didn't open my eyes, and our lips didn't break contact as he shifted, running his hand along my cheek before tucking his fingers into my hair. I broke away from him and stared into his eyes.

He was so close, his hand still around the back of my neck tucked up into my hair. He wasn't grabbing at me, pulling me toward or away from him, simply holding me, so incredibly gently. What made it even more extraordinary was I knew how strong he was. I knew he could pick me up and throw me around as though I weighed nothing, but he didn't. He displayed absolute control and restraint, and it made me feel safe in a way I didn't recall ever feeling before.

He stared at me for a beat, and when I opened my mouth to speak, he kissed me again, harder this time, the desperation thick between us. I didn't know why he needed me, what it was about me that broke the control he obviously worked so hard to maintain, but I needed him more than I'd ever needed anyone. To me, he represented everything good in this world. The parts of the world I didn't often get to see—acts of selflessness, caring and compassion, and love without only sex.

Love?

I don't know where such a thought came from, but I shoved it to the side of my mind as I pushed my tongue into his mouth, tasting him, moaning his name against his lips as I ached to have more of him. *All of him.*

Scrambling on top of his body, I pressed my chest onto his as he sank back into the old couch, groaning in protest under our combined weight. When there was a crack, and we both dropped six inches, he smirked, and I laughed with my face buried in the crook of his neck and shoulder. His arms had tightened around me when the couch had broken, and my heart swelled at the knowledge his first instinct was to protect me. The moment of laughter didn't last long when I became entranced by his scent. How it was possible for a man to smell so heavenly, I didn't know. It wasn't any cologne I had ever come across. It was pure him, and hungrily I bit into his shoulder, swirling my tongue across his skin, tasting him. His fingers gripped into my back, flexing and releasing against my skin as I kissed my way around his neck and tasted the sweet salt of his skin against my tongue. He was groaning, low and deep as I tasted his skin. The sounds he was making were intoxicating, and I wanted more. I wanted to make him *moan.*

"Zaqiel," I panted. I was practically rutting against him, grinding my hips against his, desperate for some friction, desperate for him. "Touch me, please."

His hands clenched against my shoulder blades, almost painfully. I couldn't keep still, and I didn't realize how much I needed to touch him until he was right here. Everything I wanted to say, all the hurt I was feeling from the way he ignored me these past few days, all the explanation I felt I owed him for my lifestyle until the day we met was pushed out of my mind by the feel of his hard chest underneath me and arms around my body.

When his hands glided down my back and over my ass, we moaned together as he gripped and pulled me against him. He was hard, and I could feel him through his boxers.

Hard and… I shifted my hips, *fuck*.

Good for you, Zaqiel.

He would fill me like no other man had before him in more ways than one. Because, possibly for the first time, I cared. When I sat up, still straddling him, his eyes were heavy with lust as I pulled the loose t-shirt over my head and discarded it to the side. His eyes fell to my breasts, and I gave him a moment simply to look. His lips were slightly parted as he devoured me with his gaze, and I could feel his stomach muscles tighten between my thighs. His fingers were digging into my hip bones, a good pain if there were such a thing. I ran my fingers over my nipples, and his eyes shot to mine.

"It's okay," I whispered. For some reason, he seemed to need reassurance. Perhaps he thought he was taking advantage of me, that I had some sort of fucked-up Stockholm syndrome. "I want this." And when he raised his hands, trembling slightly, and took my breasts, I gasped his name. Placing my palms on his chest, I shifted and ground my hips against his, finding that perfect spot where the outline of his cock nestled between my thighs, between my pussy lips, and I could use his hardness to grind against my clit. His hands massaged my breasts, his thumbs finding my nipples and rubbing over them as they hardened under his touch. It felt like the first time, but so much better than my first time had actually been. It felt like the way I imagined it could be, the way I wished it could always be—all pleasure and whispers and kisses.

I was so close, I had been teetering on the edge since I kissed him, and the throbbing between my legs only increased in intensity as I continued to grind against him. His eyes grew wide as he massaged my nipples between his fingers, watching where our hips met and my movement on top of him, becoming desperate and sporadic as I neared my peak.

"Zaqiel," I panted out. "I'm going to…"

I wanted to stop, to wait until we could come together, but my body was acting against my mind. The hardness of his chest under my fingers, his large hands encompassing my chest, the way his breathing was deep and ragged as though he was drawing pleasure from mine, it was too much.

I couldn't stop, and when he grabbed my chin with one hand, I stared at him.

"I want to watch you come," he whispered.

That pushed me over the edge, and as my orgasm shuddered through me, he grabbed my face with both hands, forcing me to look at him. His eyes never left mine. I struggled to keep my eyes open and in focus as he watched my expressions through the stages of my orgasm, swallowing up all the twitches and jolts from the absolute peak of intensity to the aftershocks of pleasure that pulsed through me. Just as I was coming down, he pulled me forward, hands still on my cheeks, and pushed his tongue into my mouth—urgent, desperate, hungry.

With one hand, he reached down and started yanking at my shorts, and I kicked them off without breaking apart from his lips. The sound he made when he touched between my legs and felt how wet I was, *God*, it was so *animal.* As he pulled down his boxers one-handed, I wanted to help. But every time I'd go to move away from him, he'd bite at my bottom lip and tangle his hand in my hair, keeping my face on his and his tongue dominating my mouth. My lips were swollen and raw from his constant attention on them, and all it did was make me crave more, crave the closeness that could only happen by being with him like this.

When he ran his length between my legs again, now nothing between us, he *growled*, and I swear that nearly put me over the edge again. This man, who had hesitated to touch me, who at times would barely look at me, who had done nothing but treat me with respect and care, well, he changed in that moment.

Because when he sat up, wrapping his arms around my torso, crushing my breasts against his chest, my nipples, already sensitive from his earlier attention, were aroused again at the feeling of his skin on mine. His body was hard, sculpted, and I gyrated my hips against him. When he came close to penetrating me, he growled again, nipping at my neck and shoulder and shifting me. I moaned in frustration, pleads and begs dropping from my lips. He wanted control, and I was going to give it to him—control of me and everything that I was.

He almost smiled. I could feel his lips curve against my neck as he stood, lifting me with him. Instinctively, I wrapped my legs around him, throwing my arms over his shoulders. His movements were smooth as though I weighed nothing to him, and as he lowered me onto the couch on my back and kneeled on the hard floor between my spread legs, I could finally meet his eyes again.

All the hesitation and fear were gone from his face.

His expression had darkened, and he held my hips still as I tried desperately to get him closer to me, pulling him toward me by digging my heels into his lower back.

"Please."

When his eyes met mine, I was hypnotized for a moment.

"Evie," he mumbled and leaned forward, kissing his way up from my nipples to my neck again, already red and raw from his lips and teeth.

With his hand, he guided himself into me, and I cried out, gripping his shoulder blades with my nails as I was forced to stretch around him.

Squeezing my eyes shut, I opened them when he stopped moving. His face was still buried in the crook of my neck, and his breathing was heavy like a raging bull. But he was still.

"Are you okay?" he whispered against my skin.

"Yes," I shifted my hips on the cushions. "Just adjusting."

"Am I hurting you?"

When I didn't answer straight away, I dug my heels into his back again as he went to pull out. "Don't even think about it," I said through gritted teeth.

He continued to move, slowly pushing forward until he was fully sheathed within me, and he mumbled against me, "Oh God."

His voice broke on the second syllable, and I wondered what he was thinking.

I could feel the warmth from my wetness rushing around his cock as he started to move within me, the slick pull of him inside me was too much, and I couldn't contain the moans with every slow and deliberate thrust he took.

Weaving my arms between us, I grabbed his face, much as he had mine earlier, and made him look at me. The feel of him was incredible, his weight on me, his arms on either side of my head, so I could see and feel nothing but him. Nothing existed in this world apart from us.

The pleasure was written all over his face—the

way his dark brows curved and his eyes glazed over as he struggled to keep my eye contact. I kissed him, his lips puckering to mine a split second too late as he struggled to concentrate on anything but where we joined.

He felt amazing, but I wanted more.

I *needed* more.

"Faster," I whispered against his lips.

He opened his eyes and focused on my face, then watched my expression as he pulled almost all the way out, and harder than before, slammed into me. I tilted my head back against the couch, arching up into him and hissing *"yes"* between my teeth. My fingers scrambled for purchase against the couch cushions as he hooked his arms under my knees and began driving into me. A deep growl emanated from his throat and hovered between us, almost a constant background sound to his thrusts.

I clenched and spasmed around him, and his eyes shot to mine again.

This time, there was definitely a smile.

But my mind was a mess because I was about to...

CHAPTER
10

ZAQIEL

When she came around me, and the feel of her pussy walls pulsating against my cock as I drove into her...

I think I found heaven on Earth.

She was so tight around me, and I was completely lost in her as she squeezed and gripped me. Her legs were over my shoulders at this point, and I had almost lost all control.

Almost.

I didn't want to hurt her.

But as she lay back against the couch, her legs were spread for me... for *me.* It was overwhelming, and I drove into her, relishing in the moans and cries falling from those perfect lips, swollen from our shared kisses. Evie took it *all,* everything I had to give, every inch of me stretching her open and every thrust, pushing her further down into the old couch, which groaned in protest, shuddering against the floorboards.

After she came the second time, her breathing was heavy, breaths pushed from her lungs with every thrust into her, my weight on top of her.

She was so wet, I could feel it down my thighs.

I could do this all night and day, and every fucking day until she couldn't take it anymore. Then start over again.

"You're taking it so well," I mumbled, and she moaned, louder than before.

So, she likes it when I talk to her.

I leaned forward, my lips near her ear, teasing her lobe with the tip of my tongue. "Do you like the way I fuck you, Evie?" I whispered and smiled at the way she clenched around me in response. "Does it feel good, spreading your legs and taking my cock?"

"Zaqiel..." she moaned, and I nipped at her neck. Her skin tasted so good. She smelled better than every flower in the desert and sweeter than ambrosia of the gods.

I needed to taste her.

She cried out in protest as I pulled out, but her cries were drowned again in moans as I pressed my face between her legs, hungrily lapping up her juices. She flushed with wetness again when I pushed two fingers inside her, sucking and licking at her clit.

Yeah, better than ambrosia.

Ambrosia didn't moan and twitch like that, didn't whimper and beg as I assaulted her over-sensitive clit with my tongue and fingers. With two fingers inside her, I beckoned her to come for me, rubbing my fingertips against her inner wall, flicking my tongue over her clit. When I added a third finger, pushing to get deeper, she shuddered and whimpered, and I shuddered with her. My mouth and fingers working in tandem, I brought her to orgasm again. Every sound that fell from her lips grew fire under my fingertips, and my hips rutted as I tasted her.

In one swift move, I mounted her again, penetrating her wetness at the same time as I forced my tongue into her mouth, making her taste herself on my lips. Swallowing her moans, I increased my pace, the pleasure building inside me until I was gripping the couch, the cushions tearing and almost shredded under my grip. Her surprised giggle at this reaction was cut off when I bit her bottom lip, and I grunted against her mouth when she returned the gesture.

"Evie," I mumbled.

I've never felt anything close to this, experienced anything quite like her, and her next words pushed me over the edge.

"Come for me, Zaqiel."

As I collapsed on top of her, I felt a slight ache in my knees from the hard floor.

Angels felt pain, but we mostly ignored it—trained to ignore it. But my body was sensitive to all sensations now, twitching and jerking with every aftershock of my orgasm. Still buried deep inside her, I moaned with every clamp of her walls around me. The chill of the air against my back was stinging and soothing at the same time, and her fingers gliding down my shoulders and torso left a trail of goosebumps.

I listened to her heart beat, pounding against the inside of her chest before it slowed as she came down from her high, from the pleasure that pulsed through her body and continued to squeeze every drop from me.

"Oh my God," she whispered.

I stiffened against her touch, my hands flexing against the ruined remains of the couch cushions.

God.

What had I done?

I tore myself away from her, and Evie gasped as she was left empty, her legs closing on instinct. She stared at me, those heavy eyes drowsy from pleasure, but her expression changed, morphing as mine did from a frown to wide-eyed with fear.

"What's wrong?" She sat up, levering herself with her elbows. "Are you okay?"

I covered myself with my hands, glancing around for my clothes. "I shouldn't have done that to you."

"It's okay," she said. "I wanted it too."

My cock was throbbing under my hands, wet from being inside her, dripping with her cum and mine. Panic and dread rose from my stomach to my chest, crushing my heart like a vice as she slowly covered her breasts with her hands. She could tell something was wrong, but she didn't understand what.

"Zaqiel—"

"Don't. Please don't say anything."

I scrambled to grab my clothes, reaching to where they lay near the couch and snatching them away, keeping my distance from her. This woman sat naked in front of me and had exposed herself to me in every way possible. I could see the rejection washing over her like a wave as she folded in on herself, pulled the blanket from the floor, and covered her body.

"I don't understand—"

"I shouldn't have done that. I took advantage of you. It was wrong."

"You didn't take advantage of me. How many times do I have to tell you I wanted it too?"

"It doesn't matter, I shouldn't see you like that."

"Like what?"

"Like a…" I didn't know how to find the words. I was meant to care for humanity, not feel these earthly desires and give in to them. We had shared the most carnal of desires and what was worse was I didn't regret it because she felt so good. *Too good.* The smell and taste of her skin and the connection it forged can't be faked or created any other way than through the act of…

… but now I saw her in a way I couldn't undo.

She was more than someone who needed care, more than a lost lamb to look after and send on her way. Evie was a woman. And beyond that, a woman I now felt some claim over like I owned her as if a person *could* be owned. If they could, I wanted to possess her and keep her safe from the world which I knew was more than capable of tearing her apart. I'd tear the world apart to protect her. I knew that now.

And it couldn't be because I had so many to protect and save.

I had given in to my desire for her, and these feelings stirred inside me every time I got close to her. It was beyond the physical—I'm not blind to the beauty of humans. But Evie, she drew me in as if every time she looked at me, she was beckoning me to her, every smile and laugh, every tear broke down those walls between how I thought I viewed humanity and how I viewed her.

She was special.

She was something else.

And I had given in.

I was weak.

I *am* weak.

"Like a *whore?*"

She snapped me back to reality with her words, and my mouth fell open. Her bottom lip was trembling, whether from anger or holding back tears, or both, I wasn't sure.

"No, Evie, not like that."

But she had stood and collected her clothes from the floor and held the blanket over her chest with her other hand. The flimsy blanket cascaded down her body, exposing her to me with every move she made. The situation was falling apart in front of me, and I had no idea how to make it right. Once down from the high, my first instinct was to panic at what we had done, what I had done to her, and what she had done to me just by being who she is. Simply by being an irresistible force.

But now, the panic was being replaced with fear, a fear I didn't want to admit the reason even to myself.

Because more than fear of what I had succumbed to was the fear of losing her.

"Evie, wait."

I recoiled at the way she looked at me, her

features contorted with the pain in her heart, and even as I reached out to her across the space between us, my chest opened up as her pain flooded into me.

"Don't touch me," she snapped. "I wouldn't want to *tempt* you with my body again."

She stalked past me, slamming the bedroom door behind her.

CHAPTER
11

EVIE

Tomorrow morning, I was leaving.

For the first time in a long time, I cried myself to sleep.

I don't care if he heard me or if he felt bad, he deserved to feel as rotten as I did.

Don't get attached.

Don't open up to people.

Those are the rules to living in a world such as this, being stuck in this city with nowhere else to go. Where could I go anyway? I'd only end up doing the same thing somewhere else, having to earn the trust of all the people I wouldn't trust myself.

Foolishly, I allowed myself to think I was more to Zaqiel than just another pathetic person who needed help. I don't know why he helped me. Maybe he had something fucked up on his conscience he was trying to atone for. Who the fuck knows? But I just *had* to play into the fantasy I had built in my head. Those thoughts I had allowed myself to have as he had carried me to the bath and had tucked me into bed at night, those white-picket-fence thoughts could never possibly be a reality.

He was intoxicating, strong, protective, caring, and sturdy. And I loved, *loved* I could make him smile when it seemed he never usually did.

When I kissed him that night, I knew I wasn't the only one who felt it. Those sparks you always hear about, but in the pit of my stomach, a pleasant sensation that made me think…

Home.

Yeah, I was foolish and naïve, and so stupid. I thought I was past all this girly shit, past the hope there was something out there for me better than this life. But something about him gave me a new spark, and a new hope ignited within me.

Then we had come together, and I had never felt more complete.

But it was all over too soon after the act, and the ecstasy of it faded into nothing almost straight away. I wasn't even allowed a few minutes to dwell within the false reality I had created within my mind. No, he had brought it all crashing down around me. He just *freaked out,* tearing himself away from me as though I was poison to him.

Maybe I was.

I knew what it was like to be used, but for some reason, I never expected it from him.

It hurt.

Physically, I was healed enough now. The truth was I had probably healed enough a day or two ago, but I wanted to mend the bridges with Zaqiel before I left and had to face what was outside these walls. All I had intended was to make sure we were okay after he started ignoring me.

And now, things were so much worse.

"You don't have to leave."

I pivoted on the spot, having not heard him open the door as I straightened the bed sheets. I was still wearing his boxers and t-shirt—I had nothing else to wear. I'm sure he wouldn't miss them.

"Don't you knock?" I asked flatly as I finished the corners of the bed before standing to face him. He was wearing pants but no shirt and stood with his shoulder against the doorframe and hands jammed into his pockets, looking at the floor. I couldn't see his eyes beyond the veil of lashes. Hopefully, there was guilt in those eyes.

He said he didn't want to take advantage of me, but leaving me feeling used by someone I thought cared, *that* was worse.

"Evie—"

"Thank you for taking care of me."

"Evie..." he started again, and this time when I waited, my arms crossed over my chest, he lifted his eyes to mine but still didn't speak. There was pain and guilt in his eyes, and I was glad he felt as awful as I did. But at least his pain was his own fault.

Although I wasn't entirely blameless in this situation. My pain was my fault for being sucked into thinking he might actually give a shit about me. Apparently, I was born so wicked that I enticed a man who otherwise would never have given into temptation, which said worlds about me. I was better off away from here.

"Yes?" Part of me still wanted to hear whatever it was he had to say.

That glimmer of hope was still inside me, hoping he could redeem this situation.

"I'm sorry." He looked at the floor again and couldn't seem to hold my gaze.

"Tell me what you're sorry for, Zaqiel."

He raised his eyes to mine again, and I held his stare, even though it was painful to do so. It felt like he could reach inside my mind and pull out all the darkest parts of me and make them go away. But then what would I be left with? I don't think I'd know how to function in this fucked-up world without my layers of darkness protecting me.

"I'm sorry I hurt you."

I pressed my lips together. That answer was as cryptic as everything else about him. I twirled my apartment key between my fingers. He had never hidden it from me. It was always on the bedside table. The opportunity was always there to leave as soon as I was well enough to do so. He knew as well as I that I had stayed slightly longer than required. And if it weren't for last night, would I have stayed longer?

Probably.

Maybe.

Definitely.

"I'm leaving."

He paused, then, "Okay."

Waiting a beat longer for him to protest, I moved to stride past him. When he grabbed my arm, I spun around to face him, looking into his eyes with grim determination and trying not to let the hope he kept stamping out show on my face.

I waited for him to say something.

He didn't, but he turned fully and took a step toward me.

I yanked my arm from his grip. "Goodbye, Zaqiel. Do *not* follow me."

He stopped, staying in the bedroom doorway like an obedient puppy as I backed away.

And I hated the part of me that still wished he had tried harder to follow.

It took me a moment to get my bearings once I was outside.

Christ, it was bright out here.

The apartments in this area weren't exactly known for their abundance of natural light and welcoming entranceways or open-plan living spaces, so I stood squinting in the sunlight for a few moments after a couple of weeks in the semi-dim apartment lighting.

It took me a moment longer than it should have to realize I had no shoes. The pavement was still cold from the nighttime chill, and I curled my toes against it. Everything about reality felt harsh and cruel now I had known the embrace of someone who actually cared.

At least, I thought I did. But apparently, whatever standards Zaqiel held himself to were more important than me.

I got that. I was no one special.

Crossing my arms over my chest, the cool breeze was making it abundantly clear to the world I wasn't wearing a bra either. I wasn't too far from my apartment building, a few blocks maybe, so I turned and walked briskly down the street, hoping the pace would keep me warm and the graze of the pavement on my feet would distract me from thoughts of Zaqiel.

It wasn't working.

It was quiet at this time of the morning. Those who didn't work were likely sleeping off a hangover from the night before, and most of the girls like me would be in bed, some next to strangers, some not. Although I encountered no one along the way who cast me more than a disinterested stare, I kept glancing over my shoulder at every corner, expecting Tyson or one of his goons to be there.

I better start thinking about what I'd say to them because they were bound to realize quite quickly I was back. Word traveled fast.

Making it to my apartment without incident, I called to Heidi as I stepped through the doorway. There was no answer, so she had already left. I searched around, no note. I didn't bother to check if anything was missing. I trusted her enough, and I had nothing worth stealing anyway.

Collapsing onto the bed, I sighed loudly. *What the fuck do I do now?*

I didn't want to go back to the life I had before, but what choice did I have? Maybe I could be a dancer at that club down the road. Dancing surely had to be better than hooking, but I doubted Tyson would let me go. Being with another man would feel wrong now, regardless of the fact there'd be no emotional connection, nothing but a body on a body, one paying for the other.

But I couldn't get the memory of Zaqiel's body on top of mine from my mind. The hard lines of his chest, the feel of his hips pressing forcefully against the inside of my thighs as he spread my legs and took me. While he was animalistic, there was still something so incredibly gentle about him, as though his arms around me could protect me from the world outside, and him being inside me could mend all the parts of me that were broken.

Sighing again, I closed my eyes and allowed my hand to trail down my body, brushing my fingers over my exposed stomach as I lifted the t-shirt before venturing under the elastic band of the shorts. Groaning, I touched myself, realizing even the memory of him had made me wet.

It had been a long time since I got myself off thinking of anyone in particular.

But Zaqiel, I couldn't get him out of my mind.

Banging on the door tore me from my dreams. I glanced out the window, the light barely a dim haze over the building across the street—either I had slept all day or napped for barely half an hour. Blearily, I walked over to the door, and it wasn't until I had unhooked the chain I realized I should've been more cautious about who was knocking.

The door burst open, the edge of it colliding into me even as I stepped back. I clutched my hands to my face as a splattering of blood burst from between my fingers. Collapsing to the floor, I tentatively felt my nose. I didn't think it was broken, but then again, what did I know? Instinctively, I curled into a ball and wrapped my arms around my head, and when my hair was grabbed, I was dragged to my feet, and I screamed.

"Where the *fuck* have you been?" Tyson exploded in my face.

I could barely think straight. I couldn't believe I had been stupid enough to even open the door without asking who it was. He'd have just kicked it in anyway, those little golden chains do nothing, but at least I'd have had time to move away. Maybe then I could've talked him down before he lay a hand on me. I should've known they'd be watching the building. They wouldn't use resources to look for me, but they would've been damn sure to be here if and when I got back.

"I... I don't know!" I cried.

He laughed. His sick, twisted chuckle sounded as though he was on the edge of hysteria. "You really think I'm that fucking stupid, huh?" He let go of my hair, twisting his arm so I was forced to the side and fell to the floor again. "Who was that guy who took you?"

I felt the anger building inside of me as though my stomach acid was boiling, sending waves of acidic rage up my throat. "How the *fuck* am I supposed to know, Tyson?" I screamed, matching his tone and volume. He even backed away half a step when I pushed myself to my feet. I wasn't as short as Heidi, and I'm sure the anger was showing on my face, past the blood.

Maybe the blood only added to the effect.

I hoped I looked like a fucking possessed demon to him right now.

"I couldn't see *shit* because Paul fucked up my face, *remember?*"

"Don't you yell at me, whore."

Shoving at his shoulders, I rammed down the immediate warning that sprung up in my gut that it was a terrible idea to push him. I didn't care anymore. I was sick of being blamed for being the victim. Sure, there were things I could've done differently in my life, but it wasn't my fault Paul had done what he did, and it sure as shit wasn't my fault Zaqiel had found me and then let me go just as easily.

"Fuck you, Tyson," I spat the words out. "Why didn't you help me? I could've died."

"You were fine."

"I was *fucked up*, and you just left me on the street."

"We were coming to get you, but then some asshole took you away."

I decided it was better to continue playing dumb. "Well, whoever that asshole was, he probably saved my life that night."

He almost saved my heart, too, from being ruined by this world.

Almost.

Tyson approached me, and I flinched as he raised his hand, but he simply cupped my cheek in his palm, his tone changing. "Babycakes, you know I wouldn't have let you die."

"I don't know that."

"Haven't I always looked after you?"

I glanced around the rundown apartment he paid the rent for with my money. The clothes I bought with the allowance he drip-fed me—money that was rightfully mine.

His fingers tangled in my hair, and he tugged hard. "Haven't I always looked after you?"

"Yes," I whispered, tears springing to my eyes at the pain.

Zaqiel would never hurt me like this.

But he wasn't here.

Tyson's palm returned to my cheek, slapping lightly before cupping my face, his expression softening as though moments ago he hadn't basically threatened me. "I'll ask again, sweetheart." A shiver ran down my spine. The tone he used when he called me pet names had more than a hint of danger running through it. "Where have you been?"

The tears were coming fast now, and I couldn't stop them, but it wasn't fear. I didn't care what Tyson did to me because I wanted out. Whether that meant I left or he killed me, I didn't care anymore.

I. Wanted. Out.

I didn't want to work for or near him ever again. Besides, nothing he did to me could feel worse than the rejection from Zaqiel.

"I swear, Tyson, I don't know." I choked back a sob, letting the tears come, hoping he misinterpreted them. "I was kept locked in a room. He fed me and cleaned my wounds, then just dropped me somewhere on the side of the road, and I walked home. I swear I don't know. *I don't know.*" My voice faded into a whisper and then into nothing. I closed my eyes against his touch, wishing he'd take his hand away from my cheek.

Tyson continued to stare at me and ran his thumb across my upper lip, possibly trying to wipe away the blood, most likely smearing it. My vision was still shimmering with tears when I held his gaze, green eyes that would've been beautiful in contrast to his tanned skin if they were not filled with such cruelty.

I made the mistake again of relaxing. You'd think I'd have learned never to relax around him. He patted me on the cheek, and I flinched. When he smiled, I knew I was in trouble.

"Rest for today, but just know…" he started as he turned to leave. That sneer turned wicked, a grin that promised pain. "I don't believe you don't know who he is."

I stood there trembling even as he closed the door before I collapsed to the floor again and sobbed like I hadn't done in years.

CHAPTER
12

EVIE

After showering, I dressed in jeans and a tight t-shirt. I wasn't about to wait around here for Tyson to come back and decide I needed to work again. I actually wanted to wear loose pants and a baggy t-shirt, but I still needed to dress to impress today.

Also, I had no idea where my phone was, so I'd need to pick up a replacement while I was out. I really wanted to get hold of Heidi. I still didn't know where she was, and I tried not to think about how it seemed like my apartment hadn't been lived in for weeks.

But first, I was going to get a new job.

It couldn't be just any job. I needed something that would offer protection from Tyson and his damn goons. Without it, as soon as he realized I was working elsewhere, I'd be dead as soon as I stepped out onto the street.

Weeks ago, I wouldn't have cared much.

Now, I'd seen something better, and while I might never be able to get a fucking white picket fence, I didn't want to be stuck as one of Tyson's girls forever either.

Forever, or until he decided I wasn't young and pretty anymore, kicked me out on my ass, and left me homeless.

The strip club—The Palace—was a few blocks away from my apartment building, but I still circled around the long way. I didn't want to make it too obvious to any overly observant people where I might be headed. I knew the club owner, Vina, simply from being around the block. She used to do my job until she started dancing. She now owns the club after she married the owner, and he was subsequently shot a decade later. Surely, she'd help me out. We weren't close or anything, but we tended to look after each other around here, just like I looked after Heidi. Now my hope was Vina would look after me.

I only needed a chance, just a chance to prove myself. I could dance. I used to do ballet when I was a child with one of my foster families, one of the few that actually took an interest in me. Unfortunately, they couldn't adopt me. They already had seven children and were pushing it financially as it were. I tried to understand, but I was only eight, so it still broke my heart when they had to move to Europe because of Evan's job, and I was left behind and put back in the system.

So, two years of ballet. It wasn't much, but it had given me grace and love of movement, and I never stopped practicing, although I could only improve so much without further lessons.

A chance to show them I knew how to move, and the clients would like it. I may not make as much money there as I did—theoretically, although Tyson managed it all—hooking. But that didn't matter. I needed to take my life back, and this was the only way I knew how.

I came up a side street and stopped, surveying the area before turning the final corner to the club. It was open twenty-four hours, and I'd like to say I was surprised that even at this time of day, there were customers present in the club, several of them drunk already, or perhaps *still* drunk from the previous night.

My hands were shaking. I needed a drink myself.

Finding Vina behind the bar talking to the girls there, she greeted me with a raised tattooed eyebrow. She recognized me but didn't remember my name. So, I introduced myself, shaking her hand as though this were a typical interview.

"Vina, I'm wondering if you have any openings for dancers..." I glanced around, "... or waitresses."

She scanned me, her eyes wandering up and

down my body before finally resting on my face and the bruise I'm sure was forming around my nose and eyes.

My smile dropped before she even had a chance to speak, and I saw the answer on her face. "I'm sorry, sweetie," she said, her voice dark and heavy with a hint of an accent I could never place. "Nothing going at the moment."

I felt something in me break, and I leaned across the bar, gripping the edge of it when she moved her hands out of the way. Although I'm sure I looked crazy, I couldn't help it as desperation gripped me internally. If I came out of here empty-handed and was seen, then all of this would be for nothing.

"Please." My knuckles almost turned white with my grip on the edge of the sticky bar. "I have to get out, and I have nowhere else to go. I'll do anything... cleaning, taking out the trash, counting money, I don't care. I just have to get out."

Although her expression softened, her eyebrows lowering and crimson lips turning down, the sympathy evident on her face, I knew she hadn't changed her mind. Vina understood my desperation, and she came toward me and took my wrists in her hands, stroking my arms with her thumbs.

"I'm so sorry, sweetie. I'd help you if I could. You know I would." I saw her gaze wander over the scars on my arms and bruises on my face again, but

I took no consolation of the pain in her eyes, reflecting mine. "I promise you, the moment I have something, I'll call you first. Do you have a number?"

Dragging my arms out from her grip, I mumbled my number, reminding myself to get it switched over from my old sim to my new one. She wrote it on the inside of her arm in between all the permanent inked artwork that adorned her skin.

I turned to leave when she snatched at me, taking my hand again. "Do you need somewhere to stay tonight? We've got a girl upstairs, but I'm sure she wouldn't mind a roommate for a while."

I tried to smile but couldn't and simply shook my head, muttering a thank you and turning to leave. I know Vina had a business to keep up, and she tried to help as many girls as she could, but I also knew she couldn't simply let in every stray girl who wandered her way. Because then the club would be full of girls she couldn't afford to keep, the place would shut down, and no one would have a job anymore.

I'm not sure why I thought I deserved any better than the life I had in the first place.

Try as I might, I couldn't keep the tears at bay, not even until I was walking home, and I could cry along the way in peace. No, they were streaming down my face, thick and fast as I exited, and I wiped them away hastily. Momentarily, I forgot I had bothered to put on eyeliner and mascara and cursed when it smeared on the back of my hand, and, of course, all over my cheeks.

The bouncer grabbed my arm as I went to leave.

"Let me go, Carl," I whispered, no energy left for any sort of confrontation.

"Girl, look at me."

I did, and I hated the sympathy I saw on his face. Carl was almost six foot seven, arms like tree trunks, and covered head to toe in tattoos, a large skull adorning the back of his shaved head.

But his eyes, he had the softest eyes.

I never did find out what he went to prison for all those years ago, but I did know he had a good heart with a wife and family he loved very much. He couldn't get much work other than this with his history. Who would give him a chance? But I think he liked being here, had made himself the unofficial guardian of the girls who worked here, and they loved him for it.

I'd love to have that sort of protection, but apparently, even when I thought I had it, I didn't really.

Another reason I wanted to work here—Carl

would slam Tyson's head into the bricks if he tried to get to me.

"What's wrong?" he asked.

I opened my mouth to reply, steeling myself to keep it together so I could answer his question and go home.

Instead, what happened was I burst into tears, huge raking sobs tore through my body and left me a quivering mess when he drew me against his chest with large arms, shushing me as though I were a child.

"I never used to care, you know?" I hiccupped.

"What do you mean, baby girl?"

"About me, about any of this. I didn't like it, but I just accepted this was my life, and things would never change." He relinquished his hold on me as I pulled away and wiped at the tears on my face, no longer caring about the makeup—it was ruined anyway. I raised my eyes to his, and the genuine sorrow in his face almost made me crumble again. I bit my lip against another sob that threatened to rise in my chest. "But then I saw a glimpse of the other side, you know? At least, I thought I did. What it was like to have someone look after me, someone who cared and not have to worry about the world outside. And now..." I waved my arm pathetically at the club, "... I can't go back to hooking, I just can't. But I have nowhere else to turn."

He simply watched me as all the words came

tumbling out. All the thoughts I had no one else to express to and the mixed-up emotions that had been eating away at me in what was a devastating climax over the past twenty-four hours. It all came together with Zaqiel, only to be torn apart again, before crashing back to reality in the worst way.

"I need out, and I don't know what else to do. I have no skills, no work experience, no references, and absolutely no savings. Not to mention nowhere to live or go. If I can't be a dancer, then I have to continue hooking, and I don't know if I can do it anymore. I feel like I'm dying inside, and I think I'll have to let it happen, let myself die inside because I need that darkness back so I can continue with my life how it was before, and I can pretend I hadn't seen something better."

I finished with a deep, shuddering breath and stood with increasing awkwardness as Carl continued to watch me.

"Evie, right?" he said finally.

I nodded, touched he even remembered but too exhausted to say anything.

"Look..." He glanced over his shoulder as if checking to see if anyone was listening. He slid a card from his pocket and pressed it into my palm, closing my fingers over it before I could look. "Call Leo and tell him I sent you."

"What's this?"

"It's an escort service." When he saw the hope

drop from my face, he squeezed my shoulder. "Not like that, high-end, and you rarely have to sleep with the customers. It's more about... company. Sometimes they want dates to events to impress others or just want company for the night... maybe a blow job."

He pressed his lips together at the look on my face, and I dropped my eyes to the ground. It's not like I was a prude, obviously, but hearing him explain it like it was a real job, a legitimate position that involved the occasional blow job, somehow seemed cheap.

He waited until I looked at him before Carl squeezed my arm again. "I know it's not what you wanted, baby girl, but it's better than what you do now, and it's the best I can do for you." He glanced over my shoulder. "You best get out of here now. I can't see what sort of car that's coming, but just in case it's someone looking for you, you better go."

"Thank you, Carl," I whispered, before turning and running, taking the first two corners at a fast speed and hiding out the back of the building until I heard the car pass. Carl was right—the car could've been anyone. But I couldn't risk being found talking to him or anywhere near the club, not until I had some new protection anyway.

I pushed myself off the wall I had been leaning on and moved down the street to get a new phone, thumbing through the handful of notes I had in my pocket. It would be a cheap one, but it would do, then I could make the phone call—after calling Heidi—that would hopefully be a step toward change.

CHAPTER 13

ZAQIEL

She got a new job.

It wasn't a huge change, but it was a change, and Evie was away from Tyson and, therefore, hopefully, the man who had beaten her so thoroughly. She was still in the same apartment, though, and I was concerned Tyson would eventually figure out what she was doing. He'd only put up with her turning down customers for so long, and while she wasn't his only concern, she seemed to be on his shit-list because of her disappearance. But these last two days, she had been packing up her clothes and few belongings, so hopefully, that meant she was moving, and Tyson wouldn't find her wherever she ended up.

I would, though.

I wouldn't want to take back what I did by taking

her from the street, even though she was now in trouble with Tyson because of me. I may not be proud of how I handled myself the entire time, but I was glad I had saved her life. She deserved better, especially from this city and these grimy streets.

Evie deserved better than what I could offer her.

Evie hadn't told them who I was or where I lived. Otherwise, they would've come after me. I appreciate that somewhere in her, there was enough of a break in her rage toward me not to give me up, but I almost wish she had. I wasn't afraid of those men, and if I had to attack them—in self-defense, of course—then so be it.

I had been watching her since she walked out that morning, making sure she was okay.

Of course, I was still helping other people where I could, but I'd always come back to her.

When she cried on the shoulder of the bouncer at the club, I wished it were me, then cursed myself for desiring that intimacy again. *What had she done to me?* I was a Watcher, here to help people. I never should've seen her the way I did and given into the physical attraction that pulled us together.

Physical attraction, like that's all it was, and she didn't stir other things inside me.

Certainly, I never should've considered that the feeling in the pit of my stomach when I looked at her was anything other than a natural protective instinct.

It had only been a couple of days, and I couldn't stay away from her.

Watching her now move across her small apartment, shoving clothes haphazardly into a garbage bag, I couldn't tear my eyes away.

Because every movement, every turn of her head and flick of her hair, every time the light caught on the scars on her back peeking out from her tank top, it was all painful to me.

Because every movement only made me want to touch her and feel her move under me again.

I knew I hurt her when I rejected her. So I welcomed the pain that flooded me now knowing I could only watch her from a distance.

Penance for my crimes.

Although I shouldn't be watching at all.

But whatever it was we shared, maybe that's what made her want better for herself, and if I had to live forever with this stake through my heart, I could do so.

If it meant she was safe and happy.

Maybe one day I'd forget her, and the pain would fade.

I'll add that to the list of lies I told myself lately.

She went by Candy, but her name was Margaret.

I had seen her around the area for a while now, and it took me longer than I'd like to admit to realize she was homeless. She was neither a dancer nor a prostitute and not under official protection. Although I'm sure she'd have sold favors to get some cash for food.

I had been helping her out with money and food for a few weeks. She moved around a lot, and whenever I saw her, I'd stop and sit with her on the pathway, and we'd talk. She always wanted to talk—I guess she didn't have anyone else to talk to.

She was looking for her younger brother, Tristan, who had gotten mixed up with the wrong crowd and dropped out of high school. She had left her parents' place and come to this end of the city— the *wrong* end—to look for him. Someone had seen her, and whoever they were had told her parents she was hooking and dancing, both lies at the time.

They couldn't have their daughter ruining their image, so they cut her off, left her here with nothing by the clothes on her back and her phone, which she had traded in for a less expensive model so she could eat.

Candy quickly learned a name like Margaret made her stand out, and people would quickly assume she came from money. Yeah, it was a leap, but that's the sort of people you found here. She had been kidnapped once, kept for weeks before they realized they could get nothing from her family, and thrown her back out onto the street. Now she had more memories she'd rather forget tucked under her belt.

That was three years ago.

She hadn't found her brother yet.

I suspected he had either moved on to another city with whatever gang he had been caught up in, or he was dead. But how could I tell her that? She had thrown away everything to find him, and I swear if I ever found him, I'd make sure he understood the pain she had gone through to try to bring him home. I'm sure he had his own tragic tale, but I didn't know him. He was nothing but a name in a story to me. All I saw was Candy in front of me, a hint of class still evident in the way she sat, her long legs stretched out in front of her and crossed at the ankle. She had been picking up work here and there, small chores and cleaning, anything people were willing to offload for a few dollars. Three nights a week she was able to sleep on William's couch, a young man who lived around here, when his roommate was on his weekly overnight trips for his job as a truck driver.

I knew all of this about her, and she knew practically nothing about me.

She had tried to ask on more than one occasion and learned I wasn't going to open up.

But things were different now, and I blamed

myself more than I blamed Evie.

But I wouldn't be thinking this way if it weren't for Evie.

Because I had never paid attention to Candy's body before, not the way I saw it now. Previously, I'd have assessed her, noticed she looked hungry and dirty, and offered her what she needed. I'm not blind. I could tell underneath the dirt, she had a beautiful face and beneath the rags, there was a shapely body from years of keeping fit and well but thinner now from a few years more of not always having enough to eat.

But I had never noticed the curve of her breasts, the hint of cleavage visible through the buttons straining to keep together and hide her dignity. The shirt was too small for her, but she took what she could get and often kept a jacket wrapped around herself to cover her body from passersby.

When I was around, she relaxed, and I had never before wished she didn't.

Because as she leaned back against the wall of the apartment building behind her, one of countless in the area, packing in as many people as possible into cheap living spaces, her neck curved and back arched, pushing her chest out. I noticed the way her feet trembled only slightly as she stretched her legs. I had to turn away when I found myself wondering if they would tremble in the same way if I were between those legs.

Dammit, Evie.

"What's wrong, Zaqiel?"

I turned back to Candy. She still had her eyes closed, and her face turned toward the sun with her head tilted back against the wall. "Who says something is wrong?"

A smile curved on her lips. "You're quieter than usual today, and that's saying something."

I grunted.

"It's a woman, isn't it?" she asked, rolling her head toward me.

I stared into her eyes—a hazel so light it was almost amber. "I'm not here for that."

"I know. You're a protector, blah blah blah. But whoever she is, she's gotten under your skin, so why are you here with me?"

"I'm checking in on you. I want to help."

"I'm a lost cause, Zaqiel."

"No one is."

Lifting her head from the wall, Candy studied me. "Do you really believe that?"

I looked away.

I used to before I spent so much time with humanity and in places like this, with all the worst of society and some of the best people, just struggling to get by, overlooked by everyone and suffering. Now I knew there were many people beyond salvation, who deserved to be in Hell when their day came.

Many people whose day didn't come quick enough.

Then there were people like Evie, thrust into a life that wasn't good enough for them, shrouded in a blanket of scars, inside and out, that hid from the world a heart aching to be loved.

Not loved—protected, assisted, and helped.

I wasn't here for love.

Candy's smile dropped as I cursed under my breath. After a beat, I said, "I want to help you, Candy."

"I know you do, and just knowing you want to help is enough for me." She eyed me out of the corner of her eye, looking me up and down before smirking, mostly to herself, I suspect.

I had no idea what she was thinking.

"It's not enough for me," I said.

"You can't save everyone."

She was right.

I stood and held out my hand. She stared at me hard before taking it, letting it go the second she was on her feet. We were standing much too close, and even in the warmth of the afternoon sun fighting against the chill of the season, I could feel the heat from her body. A body that was made for things I hadn't dared to dream of before Evie. I swear she pushed her chest out, so her breasts brushed my shirt, and I gritted my teeth.

Gripping her upper arm, probably harder than

necessary, I tugged her down the street.

"Where are we going?"

"Come to my apartment. You can have a shower, get some sleep, have something to eat, and rest for a bit."

"I have work tomorrow."

I stopped walking and stared at her. She was biting her bottom lip, but it wasn't concern for being late for work. Maybe before, I wouldn't have noticed the way her gaze raked up and down my body, lingering on my arms and chest and longer on my groin. I stilled as I willed my body not to respond to the vibes she was clearly letting off.

How many women had fallen for me?

How many of them had assumed I had motives other than to help and care for them?

How many times had I not noticed because I simply didn't see them that way?

I had managed to go a few days without seeing Evie for more than a few minutes here and there, not the lingering observation I wanted to do, just to see her move. It was getting painful to breathe with the distance between us. I knew I'd cave and watch her soon. I couldn't stop checking on her, and I would move silently across the rooftops every few hours to make sure she was okay before moving on to help someone else. But I wanted to stay, even though she couldn't see me, even though she didn't know I was there. I wanted to stay and watch her for hours.

But how many more times must I be reminded of Evie? Of what she had awakened in me. Of the fact that no one, no matter how my body responded, made me want to cross that line again.

Except her.

I'd do it again with Evie.

Over and over again, I would tie her to my bed and take her until we fell into an exhausted pile and the inside of her thighs were sticky and wet with sweat and cum.

The admission frightened me, made me realize I was compromised, and perhaps I was no longer worthy of doing the good work here on Earth. Because if I had succumbed to my desires once, and I *knew* I'd do it again, given a chance.

Well.

Then I was no angel.

"You won't miss work," I told Candy, keeping my voice as steady as possible.

And I simply hoped she didn't misinterpret it.

CHAPTER
14

EVIE

He found me, I don't know how he did, but I guess I knew he would eventually.

Tyson.

This time I asked who it was before I answered the pounding on the door.

This time, it didn't matter.

The door frame splintered as he used a well-aimed kick to break the lock free of its flimsy hold on my safety, and I backed away as quickly as he approached me, his hands balled into fists at his sides. But I wasn't quick enough, and where would I have gone anyway? I was at the window, my back pressed against the cool glass when he reached me, his fist tangling into my hair as he pulled me up until my face was level with his.

Pure rage.

"Evie." His voice was silky smooth, a terrifying contrast to the flare in his eyes and twitch of his fingers as he twisted my hair further into his fist. "Where you have you been, sweet girl? You left without even saying goodbye." I swallowed heavily against the bile rising in my throat as he continued, "Well, imagine my surprise when I went to find you, ready to tell you to stop turning down jobs, and your apartment was empty. I'll admit, I admire the guts it must have taken for you to leave." He licked his lips. "That bravery will come in handy when it comes to your punishment."

His thumb ran across my bottom lip as it started to tremble, and my back stiffened as he pressed his lips to mine, not moving as he kissed me, softly, delicately, before returning his thumb to my chin.

"Tyson," I gasped out. I had no idea what I was going to say anyway.

"I can't lose another girl so soon. It'll cut into my profits."

Something clicked in my mind, and I muttered, "Heidi?"

I had been trying to call her for days, but she never answered. The phone would ring out and leave me no option to leave a message, not that I would anyway. It had occurred to me Tyson had her phone, but even texts went unanswered, and if he did have her phone, a text would've been the perfect opportunity for him to pretend to be her to try and lure me out. But there was no answer from her, nothing. She was off the grid.

He smiled, and a shiver ran up my spine.

"Paul wasn't happy that Heidi was withheld from him. Not happy at all."

"What did you do?" I croaked.

"I gave her to him. He offered to pay triple, so how could I refuse?"

My stomach sank. He had killed her. I just knew he had. I thought I was going to be sick.

"Where is she?" I barely managed to get the words out without vomiting.

"I had to let her go. She's not dead," he added at the look on my face, "But Paul, he uh..." his hesitation wasn't through any guilt or sorrow, but the glee he was taking in watching my reaction as he dribbled out information, a threat in itself. "He broke her face. Now no one wants her."

I choked back a sob, my legs shaking.

Oh Heidi.

I had made things so much worse for myself in my pursuit of something better. I'd have been better off forgetting Zaqiel and going back to Tyson, accepting this was it, and nothing would ever be better. I was foolish to try for anything else.

Now I was going to pay for it.

Gasping as his hand snaked up my body, purposefully grazing my breasts before coming to rest on my throat, my eyes watered as he increased his grip against my windpipe.

"I like you, Evie, I do. So, I'm going to give you one more chance." He licked his lips. "You have until midnight tonight to be back in your apartment, or I'll send the boys after you." He snarled, "*All of them.*"

Releasing my throat and hair at the same time he dropped me to the floor, I curled into a defensive ball as he aimed several kicks at my stomach and then my kidneys as I tried to roll away. I screamed against the onslaught and cried out loud when I opened my eyes, and his face was inches from mine.

"Whatever the clients want to do, I promise it's nothing compared to what I'll do to you if you don't come back."

Either I'm a glutton for punishment, or I had an inch of hope left within me.

Or I was hoping that the client Leo had set me up with was a psychopath who would kill me and put me out of my misery.

Whatever the reason, I kept my dinner date with him.

I was able to wear a little black dress with

stockings and heels, which covered any bruises I had around my ribs and all the scars on my legs. I had long ago given up trying to hide the scars on my back and arms, and I wasn't about to live my life in a turtleneck.

I spotted him almost immediately. He was wearing a tweed jacket of all things, and honestly, my joy was genuine. Because there was something so incredibly endearing about an older gentleman in a tweed jacket. I imagined he'd wear a matching cap some days, his silver hair peeking out from underneath. He looked like a deer caught in headlights as I approached the table, weaving my way through the other tables and chairs before extending my hand out to him and tucking my clutch under my arm.

"Clive?" I asked.

"You must be Evie." I smiled at him again, trying and failing not to stiffen as he took my hand, his hold on me lingering.

Endearing in a tweed jacket, yes.

But trustworthy? I had too many experiences that taught me the failings of trusting anyone straight away.

A shadow of a frown passed across his face when he noticed my physical reaction, and I cringed internally. If he gave feedback to Leo that one of his girls was scared of being touched, then it would be over.

Who am I kidding? It would be over anyway. Tonight, I'd have to go back to Tyson.

Even Carl couldn't protect me now.

Zaqiel might be able to, but I didn't want to ask him.

Clive came around the table and pulled out my chair for me, handed me a napkin to drape across my lap as I sat, and indicated to the waiter to fill my wine glass.

We studied each other for a short while. I kept my back straight and my body as still as possible. His head was slightly cocked, and his hands twisted in his lap until the waiter left.

"First time," he mumbled.

I was about to tell him he wasn't my first client when I realized it wasn't a question but a statement.

"I'm sorry?"

"It's uh…" He looked around the restaurant, an expensive place bordering an area between the good and bad ends of the city. Perhaps so those with money could come here and feel dangerous. Perhaps so they could tell themselves they were helping, knowing the waitstaff and the valets were likely from my area. Or maybe it was the perfect place for men like Clive to meet with women like me. "It's my first time meeting with someone. Someone like you."

I smiled.

It was fake, but I smiled anyway.

"There's no need to be nervous, Clive. We're just out to dinner, to have a chat, get to know each other a bit, and enjoy each other's company."

He nodded, but his hands were still twisting in his lap.

"You're very beautiful," he said.

"Thank you."

"It's been a long time for me since I've been on a date."

"You and me both." Again, I grimaced at my response, but he chuckled, and I relaxed slightly.

"My wife died, you see. I'm just looking for some company. I get lonely." He looked me up and down but only briefly before his gaze rested on my face. "I may be old, but I'm not dead and still enjoy the company of beautiful women."

"I'm sorry to hear about your wife."

He nodded, his eyes shining. "I'm not here to use you, Evie, I mean that. I just want company, that's all."

He must have noticed my shoulders slump slightly as I relaxed further, and he smiled at me again. This time when I grinned back, it was genuine.

The dinner was wonderful, and I don't mean only the food, although I don't think I had eaten that well in... ever. Clive asked about me, and I kept my answers tactful, and although his eyes would skip over my breasts before lingering on the scars on my arms, he never asked about them. He didn't need to know the sordid details of my childhood and my life in general. So we just talked, and I listened to his stories and laughed appropriately, finding that as the date wore on, my smiles became less scripted and more natural.

It was hard to believe this was real. I was getting paid so well for this.

My face dropped as I remembered Tyson's visit earlier.

Of course, something like this would be too good to last.

Clive had stopped talking, and it took me a moment to realize I was running my forefinger and thumb up the stem of my glass absentmindedly.

"Evie?" he asked.

I sat upright. "Oh! Clive, I am so sorry. You must think I'm so rude."

"No, you just looked like you were elsewhere for a moment."

I smiled sadly at him. "I guess I was back outside with reality instead of here laughing with you."

His fingers brushed my shoulder as he reached toward my neck, and I flinched. "Who did this?" he asked.

Instinctively, my hand flew to my throat, covering the bruises I should've known would form from Tyson's warning.

"Nobody."

He watched me for a moment, and I became uncomfortable under his gaze.

"Evie—"

I held up a hand, and he stopped talking. "Clive, please. It's a dark world out there. Please, let's not ruin our date with everything that exists for me outside these walls."

He nodded, concern swimming in his eyes. But he respected my request and didn't ask about the bruises on my neck or face, nor the scars that adorned my body. I could tell they bothered him, though, not that he found them ugly or repulsive but because he wanted to help.

For some reason, he cared.

I thought again of Zaqiel.

Where were all these people who cared years ago?

Maybe I could have had a different life.

Clive had offered to walk me home, and as I made my way back through the city, I wished I had taken him up on his offer. After how nice he was, we finished the night with nothing more than a chaste kiss on the cheek and a prolonged hug. I hated to admit I was embarrassed by where I lived. I couldn't afford much, even less now that Tyson wasn't paying my rent, and my choices were so limited given Tyson's hold on a few of the landlords in the area. I didn't want Clive to see how I lived. He might want to take me in, offer to buy me a nice place, or take me back to his. I couldn't allow him to do that. I wasn't worth it.

I regretted my decision to walk alone even more when I was grabbed from behind and dragged into an alleyway.

The man said nothing, slapping me hard enough to make me hit the ground before lying on top of me, crushing me against the grime and dirt. I screamed, and he slapped a hand over my mouth, his other hand scratching painfully at my thighs, trying to create a ladder in the stockings so he could tear them. He gave up after a while and tugged at my dress hard enough to break a strap, fondling obscenely at my breast and grunting as I continued to scream against his hand and beat him with my fists.

He had successfully managed to tear my stockings and was freeing himself from his pants when the other man showed up.

Half hidden by darkness, I didn't need to see his face to know he radiated danger. But at that moment, I had no other choice. Locking eyes with him, I pleaded for him to help me, praying he would and not simply join in the attack.

Or wait his turn.

Whoever he was, he saved me.

I know what he did to my attacker. No matter how tight I clamped my hands over my ears, I could hear his screams as his testicles were torn from his body, and he was left in a bleeding pile.

My savior walked me home, and for some reason, even gave me a handful of cash. He took my breath away when he was close. He smelled amazing, and I found my legs going weak and myself getting wet despite the trauma I had just endured.

Thankfully, he was gentlemanly enough to turn me down. I don't even know why I offered anything in the first place.

I was numb as I walked up the stairs to my apartment on the fifth and top floor, but the second the door was closed and locked behind me, I collapsed.

Before this week, I hadn't cried like this in years. Now I cried every day.

Before now, I hadn't had the light within me to turn to darkness.

Before Zaqiel, I didn't know I had anything to lose.

CHAPTER
15

ZAQIEL

My shoulders shook. I couldn't take it anymore.

Every hour away from her was agony, and while I was happy she was making changes in her life, I couldn't seem to get away from the pain of not being near her. No amount of reasoning or soul searching held any answers for me, and the draw to her was too strong. My reaction to Candy had cemented what I already suspected, that this was beyond physical. Evie wasn't only a body to me, she was something more.

And I needed her.

It had been difficult watching her the past few days, but it was torture knowing she was attacked when I wasn't there to save her, and it was sheer agony watching her cry. She had literally dusted herself off when she stood and moved to have a shower, to wash away as much of the memories and pain as she could.

But no shower in the world was hot enough to wash it away.

I could take it away, though. I could heal her.

Maybe then it would soothe the ache in my heart.

I landed on her fire escape with a rattle, folding my wings against my back. The window was locked, and I was pleased about that, but it didn't take much to snap it off, the metal bending under my fingers until it gave way.

I'd fix it for her later.

Opening the window, I stepped into her apartment. It was smaller than the one she had been in while working for Tyson but no worse for wear. The entire floor was linoleum, peeling at the corners, with a thin rug under the couch and bed. It was all one room, save for the bathroom.

But I wasn't here to inspect her home.

Evie came out of the bathroom as I was heading toward it. When she screamed, I rushed to her, clasping my hand over her mouth and wrapping my arm around her waist, pulling her into me. Her eyes were wide with fear, and it hurt.

But then again, I did just break into her home after she had already been attacked once tonight.

"Shh, don't scream," I whispered. "It's me."

The fear evaporated from her eyes, replaced with anger, and she pressed her hands against my chest to shove me away. I could've held her if I wanted to, but I let her go, allowing her to stumble backward a step. She grabbed at the towel and held it close over her chest. I tried not to take in her body, but I couldn't help it. The towel barely covered her thighs, and I'm sure if she turned, I'd be able to see the curves of her ass.

"What the fuck are you doing here?" Evie hissed at me. "How did you get in?"

I ignored her second question and approached her again. The closer I got to her, the more the fire built inside me, stoked by her sheer proximity. Anger was radiating from her, and I matched it with my own. I didn't even know why I was angry. Perhaps I was angry at myself for allowing this to happen at all and for feeling anything on Earth, along with questioning everything that made me an angel so I could feel her next to me.

She stood her ground, and when we were chest to chest, she stared defiantly up at me, her eyes flicking between mine.

"Are you okay?" I whispered into the semi-darkness—the only light in the room coming from the moonlight outside and the bathroom light she left on glowing through the half-open door.

Her rage evaporated, although she was still staring hard at me.

"Why are you here?" she asked again.

"I can't stay away from you."

"And that's my problem *how?*"

I felt the anger flare inside me again. It *was* her fault, and therefore, her problem. I was never like this with any other human or woman. She was everything I admired in humanity and more, including seduction and beauty. She didn't even see the light within her, but I did. She was scarred, inside and out and needed someone to heal her.

I could be that someone.

But I shouldn't want to be.

And that was her fault.

Grabbing the back of her head, I slammed my lips to hers, pressing my tongue into her mouth even as she struggled against my grip. When Evie bit my lip, I let her go, and she took a step backward. Touching my fingers to the blood in my mouth, my face darkened as I stared at her.

Her stance shifted, and I thought she was going to run.

I caught her as she threw herself at me, wrapping her legs around my waist as I hitched her up, gripping her ass through the towel that became unraveled as she threw her arms around my neck. One of her hands was through my short hair, gripping and yanking until I tilted my head back and offered my mouth to her for the taking. I groaned against her lips, my hips grinding against her, making her whimper.

I know she could feel I was already hard.

I needed this. I needed *her.*

God help me.

I walked until her back was slammed against the wall, knocking the air from her lungs as I continued to devour her mouth, rutting against her, my erection straining to be free of the confines of my clothes. She moaned into my mouth, and I returned the sound. There were no words, and nothing could express the need I had for her right now.

After what she had been through tonight, I wouldn't have thought she'd want to be touched. I understood and respected that, despite the lingering instinct in me that I'd have to fight not to take her anyway. But with the way she was grabbing at my hair, pulling me to her, clawing against my shoulders and back, as desperate for every inch of contact as I was, I knew.

The only thing she wanted right now was to be touched.

But not by anyone.

By me.

Only by me.

Everything about this was wrong, yet I still felt it would all be right as soon as I was inside her again.

Her hands were grasping and gripping at my hair, yanking at my t-shirt, straining at the fabric, needing the skin-on-skin contact I was also craving. I lowered her to the floor, placing a palm on her chest and holding her against the wall, her eyes widening when she couldn't move from my grip. With my free hand, I yanked the towel from her, tossing it to the side before grabbing a handful of my t-shirt and pulling, impatient and full of emotions I couldn't get my head around. The fabric shredded over my back, and she bit her lip.

I almost smiled.

She reached for me, and I covered her mouth with mine again, groaning at the feel of her breasts against my chest and her thigh as she lifted a leg over mine. The warmth between her legs had my knees buckling. She was gyrating against the bulge in my pants as I ground against her, pressing her against the wall.

"Zaqiel..." she whispered, her voice a gasp next to my ear as I sucked on the delicate skin of her neck. I didn't want to hear it, so I placed a hand over her mouth, feeling the vibrations of her moans as I worked my tongue down her collarbone and over her nipple. There was nothing that could be said— no words existed on this earth that could completely describe our need and connection.

Evie was panting against my palm, the hot air dampening my hand over her mouth by the time I undid and tugged my pants down, kicking them out of the way. She immediately grasped my cock between her hands, and I hissed through my teeth. Grabbing her ass again, I pushed her against the wall, hovering my erection over her wet entrance while she mumbled obscenities, begging to be filled.

By me.

Only me.

I guided myself inside her, groaning as her tight passage squeezed my length. Keeping my palms on her ass, I moved her up and down on me, using her to draw out my pleasure.

I was breaking almost every goddam rule, but *Christ,* she felt too good to stop.

When she wrapped her legs around my waist, taking me fully, I shuddered, and she ran her nails down my back. The room was filled with nothing but the sounds of skin on skin, my grunting, and her moans as my hips slapped against her inner thighs with every deep thrust.

I was barely holding on to my control, gripping her almost painfully.

And she was taking it, all of it.

Fuck.

Shifting the angle slightly, I groaned again when she cried out at the pressure on her clit, rubbing in time with my thrusts. I felt a rush of warmth as she got wetter, and I knew she was close. I shuddered again because knowing I was making her feel this way and bringing her there, making her surrender those sounds from her lips was the sweetest pleasure.

I remembered her taste on my lips and tongue that night I had her on the couch, and I wanted to taste her again too. I wanted to take her over and over, to live my life in the heaven between her thighs.

Her cries took on a new pitch, and she clenched as she came around my cock. But I didn't stop, I couldn't, and showed no mercy with the pace at which I pounded into her. Her disjointed moans and cries only fueled me to go harder and faster until I thought I might break her.

Holding her up was no trial, no strain at all, and I found a rhythm coupling my thrusts with moving her up and down on me, every time bringing our bodies together and making her cry out again at the stimulation on her already sensitive clit.

With a shout that elicited complaints from her neighbors through the thin walls, I came inside her, continuing to thrust slowly, my arms trembling as I held her over me as I rode through the waves of my orgasm.

CHAPTER
16

EVIE

His grip on my ass was almost painful, and I was sure there'd be angry red marks where his fingertips dug into my flesh.

But I didn't care.

Stroking his back, I rested my chin on his shoulder as he continued to twitch and shudder through his high. I gripped him with my heels as he took a few steps backward, collapsing back onto the bed with me on top of him. When he pulled his cock from me, I sighed, only a bit sore at the pace he had taken me. But the resulting orgasm was worth it—so intense I thought I might have drawn blood on his back with my nails. If I did, he had said nothing and showed no signs of pain.

Sitting up, I watched his face, straddling him as he lay beneath me, his hands still on my hips and eyes closed. I couldn't ignore the slight frown that seemed permanently etched on his dark brows. Whatever he was battling was still going on, but he wasn't the only one with battles going on inside the mind.

He had broken into my home, and I couldn't bring myself to tell him to leave. Because no matter what happened after, he had come back to me and had taken me with more passion than he had the first time we were together.

I wondered if it would always be like this with him.

However long always was.

When he opened his eyes, his frown deepened as he saw mine, but I couldn't bring myself to wipe the expression from my face. It would feel like a lie not to let it through. Because the truth was I didn't know what he was going to do now. For all I knew, he'd reject me again, disappear into the night, and only come back when he wanted to fuck. I didn't want to be his booty call.

I needed to know what this was because it felt different. It felt real, and if this were something worth fighting for, then I'd fight. If not, I would give up, go back to Tyson, accept my fate, and hopefully, time would make me numb again.

Zaqiel had lifted himself onto his elbows and was watching me intently as though he was trying to follow my thought process. Or perhaps figure out his own. When I reached to touch his cheek, he didn't stop me, but I could see such pain in his eyes at the contact, I almost drew my hand away.

"What is it you're fighting?" I whispered.

He just shook his head with that frown still in place.

When he opened his mouth to answer, I swear I could hear my heart shatter. Because I knew before he spoke, he was going to reject me again. Whatever it was holding him back, it was too strong, or he was too weak to fight it, and being with me now was a temporary break in his resolve.

So, if this is how it was to be, I didn't want to hear it.

I pressed my fingers to his lips, and the pain in his eyes magnified, the blue of his irises almost shimmering as he watched me, never taking his eyes from mine.

"Don't," I whispered, hating the emotion rising in my chest and making me have these feelings when before him, I was so strong. "Just don't."

He sat then, his legs still on the edge of the bed and me on his lap as he wrapped his arms around my waist, resting his head against my breasts. I stroked his short hair, and when I felt his fingers tracing the lines on my back, I froze again.

He couldn't see the scars. How could he see them with how he was sitting?

He was tracing them from memory.

He had memorized me—all the lines of my body—as I had his. I had been dreaming of him. He haunted the corners of my mind every minute, and it seems I had done the same to him.

What could be so terrible that he'd turn me away again?

Was it me? Was I both the sin and the savior to him? Was I the temptation and the thing that disgusted him, where he wanted me but didn't *want* to want me? I was tainted, broken, and scarred inside and out. I was the left behind, the betrayed, the forgettable, and an empty shell of a woman in a body he lusted after.

At least with this realization, I could feel myself growing numb again.

His arms tightened around me, and that only made it worse.

I shifted until he was inside me again. He was still hard, and I moved slowly, lowering my hips until he was fully seated within me, and we sighed together. He shuddered again as I lifted my hips, riding him gently, slowly, taking every inch of him inside me and almost all the way out again. As I felt my pleasure building, his grip on my shoulders became almost painful. He had his arms around me, bent at the elbow, and his hands resting on my shoulders, pulling me down onto him with each thrust.

As he increased the pace, I began bouncing on his lap. I took his face in my hands and pressed my lips to his, holding the kiss while I rode him. My thumbs grazed the slight stubble on his cheeks, his full lips moving against mine. When I opened my eyes and looked into his, I wanted to see them glazed with pleasure, intoxicated by me.

But there was still pain there, more than there had been before.

Pressing my cheek to his, I moaned as I clamped around him. Despite my heart shattering, the pleasure of him was undeniable. Not wanting him to see the tear I could feel running down my cheek, I kept my chin on his shoulder.

If this were to be the last time, then I'd make the most of tonight.

CHAPTER 17

ZAQIEL

We fell asleep together after making love into the early hours of the morning. Even in my mind, I didn't want to call it fucking—it sounded too crude for what it was—although we were more animal than not a few times. When she bent over in front of me, my hands trembled as I grasped onto her hips and penetrated her from behind. She fit so perfectly around me, and when she fell forward into the sheets, crying out as she came around my cock as I pounded her into the mattress, I almost forgot what I was on Earth for.

Because surely nothing was better than this.

I woke early to find her leg draped delicately across mine, one of her arms across my chest, and the other twisted underneath her. It looked uncomfortable, but the soft sound of her sleep that blew the hair from her face with every outward breath indicated otherwise. I kept my one arm around her, absentmindedly tracing the lines of her scars I knew so well with my fingertips, my other hand resting on top of hers on my chest.

She looked so peaceful.

Why did this have to hurt so much?

Angels, we were supposed to be pure. To be above lust and desire, to be unable to be seduced by money and power and the creature comforts people surrounded themselves with, but she was my ultimate weakness. A wilted flower I knew I could bring back to life because I could see the purity and light that still lived within her when we were so close, we were almost one.

This world had given up on and forgotten her, and I couldn't get her out of my mind.

Or out of my heart.

She had destroyed me.

A bubble of anger was forming in my stomach, fueled by the warmth of her body next to mine. I had wanted to talk to her last night, but she had silenced me and turned me to sin again with her body I now knew so well. Every dimple and line, every scar and smooth curve—I could draw her form with my fingertips and my eyes closed. There was a battle raging inside me, and when I had wanted to get it out, to tell her what I was feeling and maybe even tell her *why* this was so hard for me, she hadn't wanted to hear it.

Still, Evie slept, clinging to me as though she wanted me to stay.

And what if she did?

That just made it harder.

Because there were so many people who still needed protection. I had left Candy in my apartment to come here. She needed help, too, as did her brother if he was still alive. There was a young man in the apartment below mine fighting a drug addiction, and every time he'd get close, his dealer would show up at his door, and he'd fall to his knees and back into the cycle. I needed to remove the dealer from the equation, not kill him, of course, but only to get him away so this young man and many others could heal.

Perhaps put the fear of God into him.

My work here would never be done, and while people fought and starved and died, I was lying here, naked and worn out from having sex all night with someone who I should be protecting, no less than I should be protecting the others.

It wasn't fair to be angry at her, I was angry at myself for allowing this situation to become so tangled and consume us both.

I had to get out of here.

Evie woke as I tried to untangle myself from the sheets and her limbs.

"You're leaving," she said. It wasn't a question.

I nodded. "I have to go."

Pulling my pants on, I wanted to look away as she sat up, pulling the sheet with her and covering her chest. I wanted to look away, but I couldn't. She glanced out the window. It was still dark, and the apartment building across the street was black. There was that glow the mornings get when the sun was only an hour or so away, a warmth to the horizon, barely visible over the neighboring buildings. She was so beautiful. I thought it every time I looked at her and even when I wasn't. Her beauty stayed steadfast in my mind even when I was desperate to look away to save what was left of my soul.

I'd seen some messed-up shit since being on Earth, witnessed more than I thought my heart could take.

But the empty resignation on her face, that was something else. She knew I wouldn't stay, and I couldn't figure out if that hurt more or less than breaking her heart. How could I explain to her how hard this was for me?

That bubble of anger flared inside me again. I wouldn't have to explain it if I were better. I wouldn't even be in this position if I had better control over myself and I hadn't fallen for her.

Is that what had happened?

I was weaker than I thought.

"I have to go," I growled, looking around for my

shirt then remembering I had torn it in half in my haste to be next to her naked body last night.

"You ruined me, you know?" she whispered.

I could feel the frown on my face, but I couldn't help it. "What?"

"You ruined me." When she raised her eyes to mine, there wasn't pain there, only anger to match my own.

"I'm sorry."

She laughed, a single loud sound that was unnatural to her. I had heard her laugh, and it didn't sound like that. She threw the sheet off her, either forgetting or not caring about her nudity, and stormed around the bed, crossing the distance between us and pressing her finger into my chest. "You're *sorry?* You're *sorry* for what you've done?"

I backed away from her, and she advanced until my back hit the opposite wall. She was too close, and the warmth from her was unbearable. Even with the rage written across her face, I still wanted to hold her. This realization flared my anger in response to hers.

"What *I've* done?" I cried. "You changed me!" Her hand dropped from my chest, and her mouth hung open, but she didn't respond. "It's not supposed to be like this," I raged. "I'm only supposed to care about you to protect you, to give you a better life. But you, *you,* got under my skin, and I saw you as a *woman,* saw you as absolute *perfection,* and now I want nothing more than to protect you as my own. Not out of duty but because I *want* to."

Evie threw her arms up in frustration. "What the fuck is wrong with wanting that?"

"It's not meant to be like this! Angels don't do this!"

She scoffed. "Angel, huh? Angels like you? Angels who are just so damn good and pure they can't possibly be spending their time with someone dirty like me."

"It's not like that."

"Do you think you're the only one who's suffered because of *this*?" She moved her hand in the space between us. "Because do you know what *you* did to *me?* You showed me what it was like to be cared for, to have someone who really cares, to have someone who I could talk to and laugh with, something I've *never* had before. You showed me all of this, all the things I didn't know what it was like to miss, but then you fucked me and rejected me. How do you think that makes *me* feel, Zaqiel?"

"I never meant to hurt you."

She scoffed again, bordering on a humorless laugh. When she raised her eyes to mine, there was rage, defiance, and a streak of resignation that cut me up. "You hurt me in a way that doesn't leave scars, and I'd go through everything I did that left me looking like this if it meant I didn't have to feel that way again."

"I'm sorry. I ruined us both. You won't see me again."

Turning, I left.

Simple as that.

I just walked away.

And she didn't call after me.

I wish she had because the growing ache in my chest was only increasing with every step I took away from her. If she had called, I'd have been too weak to say no.

CHAPTER
18

ZAQIEL

Exhaustion was raking over my body by the time I stepped foot in my apartment. The emotional toll apparently took as much, if not more, out of me than the physical toll. While the walk home in the dawn chill had reinvigorated me somewhat, there were some things that even my accelerated healing powers couldn't deal with.

"Well, well, well. Look who's home."

My shoulders slumped as I closed the door behind me. I had forgotten I had offered Candy to stay the night after having a shower and something to eat. I told her I'd be back last night when I had gone to check on Evie, but I had been distracted.

Candy had a smirk plastered on her face, and it did nothing but irritate me.

"Who is she, Zaqiel?" she asked.

"No one."

She had one of my t-shirts on and nothing else. I could see her clothes drying over the back of some chairs. Evidently, she had washed them in the shower. When she approached me, I could see she was naked underneath the t-shirt as she walked, and she grinned when she saw me looking, not stopping until we were chest to chest.

"Bullshit. You smell like sex and sweat, and you look like shit. You've been up all night fucking."

"I wasn't—"

"Hey, I'm not judging. I'm just wondering what a girl has to do to get that sort of attention from you."

I stuttered my way through asking what she meant, and she simply smiled coyly and walked her fingers up my bare chest. "You can't pretend you haven't thought about it, about fucking me, and I've *certainly* been thinking about it." Her eyes did a sweep of my body before coming to rest on my chest. Candy wasn't looking me in the eyes, only my body. It wasn't a nice feeling. "Your body is amazing, and I'd love to feel that cock of yours inside me."

I grabbed her hand. "No, I'm helping you. That's not what this is about."

She smirked as I grunted when she grabbed at my cock through my pants, gripping. "How about you let *me* help *you*?"

Stepping away, I pushed her hands from me, and she tried to undo my pants. "No, Margaret."

She pouted. "Don't call me that."

Stepping back as she moved forward again, I grabbed her shoulders and held her at arm's length. "I said *no*. Now please, let me get some sleep. I'll take the couch."

"So what did you bring me here for then? You're not even man enough to use me."

"I'm trying to help you."

"I don't need your fucking help."

Sighing when she finally turned away after glaring at me and returned to the bedroom, I collapsed on the couch and let the exhaustion take over.

For the first time in a long while, I woke up comfortable. I felt warm and protected and at home.

It didn't take me long to realize why.

My wings were out, curling around me as if cocooning me from the outside world. They were a part of me but magical all on their own. It was hard to have them folded away all the time as though I had lost a limb or had one arm tied behind my back constantly. In the early morning light, the dark grays appeared lighter than they were, each large feather reflecting the light differently.

It felt nice to be whole again.

I was shaken from my comfort when there was a bang from the bedroom, and I realized why my wings were out.

Something was wrong.

My body had responded before my mind, wrapped up in my exhaustion, and my senses hadn't been as sharp. But my otherworldly sense had, my wings unfolding and surrounding me, protecting me from any lurking danger.

I stood, leaving my wings out.

Something was going on in the bedroom. I feared someone had broken in through the fire escape and was hurting Candy, so crossing the room in a handful of strides, I stopped myself short of kicking the door down. Slowly, I turned the knob and peered into the room through the crack.

Folding my wings away, I stepped into the room. "What are you doing?" I asked coolly.

Candy whipped around, accidentally dropping the drawer to the ground she had been riffling through. My eyes did a sweep of the room before resting on Candy again.

She looked afraid.

She should be.

The room had been turned upside down, and it didn't take a sixth sense to figure out she was looking for money or anything valuable she could sell.

"Zaqiel, I—"

"I brought you into my home, offered you sanctuary, and this is how you repay me?" My voice reflected the coldness I felt inside. It was another reminder that it was becoming increasingly difficult to give humanity the benefit of the doubt.

"You rejected me," she spat.

"So you're robbing me?" I almost laughed.

Candy straightened, defiance in her face. She was so sure she wasn't doing anything wrong and was justified in her actions, all because I wouldn't sleep with her. I shook my head—that logic made no sense. But then again, I had learned some people could twist the truth around in their minds and convince themselves that no matter what, they were righteous.

I didn't pick Candy for one of those people.

Her motives for coming to this end of the city had been pure. Had she been corrupted by the darkness in this world, or was there always darkness residing within her? I had allowed many people to stay the night in my place, homeless men and women of varying ages and races, people who were down on their luck and simply needed someone to show them some kindness.

Not one of them had tried to rob me.

"You disappoint me," I said.

"Oh, fuck you, Zaqiel, like you're so fucking perfect."

"Get out of my apartment."

"Fine." She kicked a book across the floor like a child throwing a tantrum, and I stepped aside, keeping my arms crossed over my chest as she snatched her clothes from the back of the chair. When she was at the door, she turned and looked at me, the defiance replaced with a pout and wide innocent eyes. She blinked at me a few times, keeping the pout planted firmly in place. I cocked an eyebrow at her, and the expression evaporated, replaced with indignant rage. She slammed the door behind her.

I sighed and went about cleaning up the mess she left behind. Hopefully, it would distract me from the mess *I* left behind.

CHAPTER 19

EVIE

The cheap vodka probably helped, as I must have fallen asleep eventually.

At least I was numb again.

It occurred to me as I lay in the place between sleeping and waking that Tyson hadn't come for me. He said if I didn't go back to him by last night, he'd send the boys after me, but no one had come. It sounded like a blessing, but I had a horrible feeling it was a trick, and the consequences now would be much worse than if I had just given in and returned yesterday.

But yesterday was gone, and Zaqiel was gone, along with any hope I had left in whatever remained of my heart.

When I woke, I started drinking again. I'd never been a huge drinker, so my tolerance was quite low.

Half a bottle later, and I was swaying. Sitting in the middle of my mattress, it took me longer than it should have to realize I had let the bottle go loose in my fingers, and it was spilling out onto the sheets.

Whatever.

I welcomed the numbness.

I could live like this, drink myself into a stupor, and go back to work for Tyson. Maybe someone would kill me, or I'd drink myself to death. Maybe the scars would all eventually catch up to me, and one day it would be one scar, one injury too many, and my body would give up.

I was responsible for the marks on my wrists—it had been my attempt to get out.

Social services had wanted otherwise, hospitalizing me and keeping me under surveillance before removing me from that home. Then they shunted me from that home to another, and another, repeatedly until I was eighteen and could leave the system. Not all foster families were bad. Some of them were truly caring and kind and wanted nothing but the best for the children they took in. I know these homes existed because I heard about them.

Unfortunately, I didn't land in many of those homes.

The scars on my back were from my last foster father, who favored a collection of whips, belts, crops, switches, and canes—things I'm sure would be sexy in the right hands. In the wrong hands, they were nothing but pain and gouged the skin from my back until the welts turned into snow-white scars covering my already pale complexion.

One of the girls once asked me why I didn't fight back.

I was only a child, forced to grow up faster than I should have and accept the world was a dark place full of dark people. Compared to that man, Tyson was a saint to me, taking me in and giving me a place to live I could call my own, even if it really wasn't. In return, all I had to do was have sex with some strangers. Fair trade, right?

At least the sex was consensual.

Most of the time.

Sometimes it was even good.

The rest of the scars, well, they each had their own story. Almost my entire body was a book waiting to be read, but surely if anyone knew all the stories, they wouldn't believe it was possible to be about one person.

Lifting the bottle of vodka before taking another painful swig, I toasted to myself for being alive.

Clive entered my thoughts, and I wondered if his offer to look after me was still open if that's what he had meant between the lines. Maybe I'd take him up on it, and we could keep each other company. I could look after him as well—learn to cook better, wear a swing dress and heels all the time, keep the house clean, and be the fucking image of domesticated bliss. I'd never had someone to look after before, not really.

I'd tried to look after and protect Heidi and look how that had turned out.

He broke her face. Now no one wants her.

Now I didn't even know where she was so I could say I was sorry.

These thoughts were getting too deep.

Better drink some more.

I'm amazed I could get my phone out and unlock it, let alone locate the phone number and call. Clive answered on the third ring, and I pressed the phone to my ear until it hurt.

"Evie, how are you, my dear?"

"Clive!" I cried, the sob heavy in my voice. "I'm so sorry."

His tone changed in an instant. "What's wrong? Are you hurt? Evie?" He continued to call through the phone as I sobbed against my hand, dry sobs that heaved at my chest, making it ache more than it already did.

"I'm sorry," I repeated. "I don't know why I called."

"Are you drunk?" There was no judgment in his tone, and I guess the slurring of my words was stronger than I thought. I lifted the bottle and swirled the remnants in front of my eyes. Guess I had drunk more than I realized. Oh well.

"Evie…" His voice was so gentle. Why was he being so gentle with me? Why didn't he judge me for being in this state and hang up? Who was this man, and why did I even deserve to be talking to him? "Tell me where you are and let me come get you."

"No, no, no, no…" I let my words trail off, slurring into silence, "You're too good, and I'm no good. I'm sorry. Your wife must have been wonderful. I'm sorry."

"I'll come and get you. Please, tell me where you are."

I gave him my address, and he promised to be right over.

God, what a mess I was, reaching out to a client I'd only met once to come and save me from my sorrows. What was I expecting him to do? To pat me on the shoulder and tell me everything would be okay? Maybe I'd suck his cock to say thank you for his kindness. There had to be something I could give him so he would keep me around. I wasn't worth it otherwise.

Falling back onto the mattress, I felt the bottle roll from my fingers and hit the floor with a hollow clunk. The ceiling was spinning.

The silence pounded against my ear drums.

Then Tyson came for me.

Any other place, and I'm sure someone would've stopped him.

But someone of Tyson's size, carrying someone like me over his shoulder down the street in broad daylight, here, people didn't give a shit.

I was thankful for the numbness, both physically and mentally.

When I pounded on his back, managing to slur out the words that I was going to vomit, he dropped me to the ground in time, so I could get it out of my system. My head was spinning as I sat up, and I clutched it.

Then I did something stupid.

I tried to run. But I was unsteady on my feet, the purge not having gotten rid of enough of the alcohol that was already well and truly absorbed into my system. I made it two steps before Tyson grabbed the back of my top and slapped me so hard, I fell again before he hoisted me back onto his shoulder. I thought I saw the blurry outline of a couple of people across the street who witnessed the episode, but they did nothing.

When he had come into my apartment, he hadn't said a word, and after a slap across the face, I had simply allowed myself to go limp and let him pick me up. He was mumbling something about something I did and some contacts I must have. I had no idea what he was talking about, so I didn't respond.

Guess there were consequences to wanting a better life, after all.

CHAPTER
20

ZAQIEL

After I left her for a second time, I told myself I'd stay away from Evie, and I guess technically I was. I wasn't going after her directly, but I was lingering in the area, going to all the places I associated with her in my quest to find the next person who needed a leg up in life.

I found myself at the bar across from where I had found her in the street.

She wasn't there.

Why would she be? It was barely midday.

Yet there were people milling around, sticking to the edges of the room where they could hide in the dank shadows and pretend it wasn't the middle of the day and should be somewhere else. The people who lined the bar kept their heads down, focusing on their drinks and their own misery. Many of them looked like they had slept in their clothes, but none of them looked as though they were homeless. Given what I knew about Evie, I'm guessing this was a place where girls and clients alike hung out, overlooked by the pimps and goons who ran the area.

When I saw the girl at the table, my breath was sucked from my body.

She was petite, so small and fragile she looked as though she could be broken easily.

And looking at her face, someone already had in the very worst way.

At least she had gone to the hospital, but I don't suppose she had a choice. I couldn't be sure what the weapon of choice was, what type of blade or razor, but whoever had done this to her hadn't held back. Her cheek had been split from the edge of her lips almost to her ear, and then again straight up and down her face, mercifully skirting around her eye. She still had the stitches, and the doctors had obviously done their best to bring the torn pieces of her face together. But her cheek caved in around the cut, and she'd never be the same again.

Once again, my heart shattered.

Beyond the scarring she'd have, she was beautiful, with wide, innocent eyes and lips I'm sure once held a stunning smile. The scars didn't make her ugly, she was still beautiful, but she had no light in her eyes. I wondered what I'd need to do to bring that light back. For just a moment, she took my breath away enough to push Evie from my mind.

I slid into the booth across from her, keeping my distance when her hand holding her drink began to tremble, clinking the ice in the glass against the sides as a soundtrack to her fear.

"Hi, what's your name?" I asked.

"It's Heidi, but please, you have to leave," she whispered, her eyes darting around the bar.

"I was just—"

"No, you don't understand. I'm not working anymore. If you want a girl, you'll need to see Tyson."

"I only... wait, Tyson?" I was snapped out from behind the mask I had put on, the one where I was the caregiver I was before. Before Evie. "You work for Tyson?"

"I did. I don't anymore." Her hand lifted as though she was going to touch her face, then dropped back to the table.

"Do you know Evie?"

Her round eyes went wider, if that was possible, and she stared at me. "Is she okay?"

Something dropped in the pit of my stomach. "Why do you ask that?"

Heidi started twisting her hands together, resuming her sweep of the bar and every person inside it. If she used to work for Tyson, perhaps he still had people watching her. Perhaps even when they no longer worked for him, they weren't truly free.

"Who are you?" she asked, leaning across the small table.

"Zaqiel. I'm... a friend."

Her jaw dropped as she assessed me. "You're the one, aren't you? You're the one who took her?"

I hesitated. "Yes." Snatching her hands before she could pull away, I leaned to her. "Please, why did you ask if she was okay? Is she in trouble?" Heidi's lip trembled, and I squeezed her hands. "Heidi, I'll protect you. I'll take you to my place right now, and you'll be safe, but you have to tell me."

"They set her up," Heidi whispered.

"How?"

"When she didn't go back to Tyson last night after he gave her the chance, he sent someone to hurt her, but something went wrong, and the damn goon got hurt. Now Tyson is fuming."

My blood ran cold. The rapist, it was a setup. While I was helping Candy, who ended up taking my help and throwing it back at me, Evie was being attacked. If it weren't for Frank, who knows what would've happened to her.

I had a pretty good idea, and the coldness in my blood began to boil, and a white-hot rage rushed across my vision. I had to force myself back into the moment, so I wouldn't crush Heidi's hands in mine.

"How do you know this?"

She glanced around again. Her eyes seemed to never stop moving around the bar. "Us girls, we talk, you know? And even though I'm… no longer working, I still hear things." She stuttered through the next sentence when I stared hard at her. "I'm sorry, I didn't know Evie had someone who was looking out for her. Otherwise, I'd have told someone. It was planned, so there were several of Tyson's guys. One would rape her and let her go, then when she made it to the next street over, there'd be another one, and another…" There must have been a change in my face as her voice trailed off, mumbling something about putting *a train* on Evie.

I didn't need to know the ins and outs of all the terminology to figure out what that meant.

A night of torture for her, one attacker after the other.

"Where is she now?"

Her eyes filled with tears. "Probably with Tyson, if not willingly, then…"

I stood, holding my hand out. "Come with me."

With more hesitancy in her eyes, coupled with a touch of resignation that still tugged at my chest, she took my hand and shrugged. "What more can you do to me, right?"

"I'm not going to hurt you, Heidi."

She studied me. "I believe you." And as I led her out the door, checking behind me to make sure we weren't being followed, she added, "But I've been wrong before."

CHAPTER
21

EVIE

So, I guess this was how I died.

At Tyson's hand.

Not at all shocking, but still, a bit of a bummer.

My head was still spinning from the vodka and starting to ache, although I'm sure that was more due to the slap and the subsequent knock to the head than the alcohol. Maybe the alcohol was even helping, who knows. I was in Tyson's office because all good managers need an office.

It was an apartment, slightly less shitty than my old one, but twice the size and on the top floor, so the views were spectacular. I had a lot of time to admire the views as the chair I was tied to was facing the window, the sunlight streaming in and highlighting all my scars, scars which I'm sure would be added to before long and before my untimely demise. What a shame. Another young life lost at the edge of the city, where you can get your thrills and life is cheap. Well, at least I knew what love might feel like even if it was only for a while. Better than what it would've been if I had died without ever having met Zaqiel.

Although I couldn't help but think I wouldn't be in this position if I hadn't have met him. Sure, I might not have had that moment of happiness, but I also wouldn't have gone in search of something better. I'd have lived out my life, or at least the rest of the time I was young and pretty enough to sell, in perfect contented misery and numbness.

Flexing my hands against the arm of the chair, I tested the binds again, although I knew it was useless.

The apartment was empty. He'd gone to *deal with some business*, whatever the fuck that meant. But he had laughed. At least he knew I'd be here when he got back, he said.

So, I had a lot of time to think.

Too much time.

I wasn't unaware of my mortality, but being faced with it now, I felt a steady stream of fear pumping through my veins.

I wanted to live.

I wanted my Zaqiel back.

Before he even laid a hand on me, I was crying. Sitting in that chair, alone, all I could think of was Zaqiel and what a wasted opportunity it was. I'm not saying I was wrong to be angry, but I don't know, maybe we could've talked through it or some shit, something like what normal couples do.

He *cared* about me—what a rare thing to have lost.

So, part of me, some sick twisted part that craved the numbness still, was thankful when the pain started. Tyson surprised me. He said he wasn't going to kill me because there was still money to be made from me. He was, however, going to teach me he owned me, and I was nothing more than his property—mind, body, and soul.

And once I healed and recovered, I'd be put back to work and be thankful for it. Even if he had to tie me to a bed in the hotel and sell me to those who wanted a ragdoll, I would be put back to work.

For the third time in as many minutes, Tyson slapped me across the face. Hard enough this time that the chair tipped over, and without the use of my arms, I was left to hit the floor, breaking the fall with my shoulder and temple. Tyson had two men in the room, and they wasted no time in picking me up and setting the chair straight so Tyson could continue.

Poor man was rubbing his wrists. "Are you okay? Did you hurt your hand?" I asked Tyson.

Stupid, I know.

"You always were a pain in the ass, Evie." He sneered and hit me again, and I spit a mouthful of blood onto the floor. I don't know if it was the fear pulsing through my veins, the adrenaline, the fight-or-flight response burning in me, or the alcohol. Or all of it. But after he said he wasn't going to kill me, that hope flared inside me again. He may have been lying, I know, but apart from shattering me harder than I had been before, Zaqiel had shown me one thing—there was something in life worth fighting for.

One way or another, if it took me one or ten or twenty years, I'd get away from Tyson.

I would never stop fighting.

Whatever punishment he had for me today, I could take it. I'd heal and deal with the pain. Because I always did.

I smirked. He better watch his back because I'd be coming for him.

"What the fuck are you grinning at, whore?" He gripped my cheeks painfully between his fingers, forcing me to pout and tilting my face up to his.

Look, I know it was stupid, but I did it anyway.

I spat blood in his face.

The tears started streaming down my cheeks again, even as I smiled through the fear. Because his laugh was more terrifying than anything he could've said as he rolled up his sleeves.

CHAPTER 22

ZAQIEL

Heidi was safe in my apartment, and I was confident no one had followed us. It would've been much quicker to fly her there, but there's no way I could've hidden that from her.

I know I should've been more concerned about the fact it was broad daylight, but Heidi suspected Tyson would've taken Evie to his place, and I was barely containing my rage. When I had closed my apartment door behind me, the door handle had bent under my grip, and I just hoped Heidi didn't try to open it because she might think I had locked her in and was keeping her prisoner. Although, she'd be safer there than out on the streets.

Right now, there was nothing in me but the burning need to get to Evie. She had consumed me, every part of my body and mind belonged to her, and no one was to touch her but me.

Tyson had threatened to hurt her, *and* he had sent someone to attack her.

It would take everything in me not to kill him.

He had *my* Evie.

I knew I should be staying away from her. I knew *all* the things I was and wasn't supposed to do, but all of that had been thrown to the side when someone had tried to hurt her. Twice I had walked away, and each time I had felt that tug at my chest to pull me back. This time I wouldn't be walking away. All the guilt was held within me at not being there when she needed me, and not to mention all the times before we had even met when she needed someone to care for her, and she had no one but people wanting to hurt and exploit her.

This ends now.

She was mine. *Mine.*

I *should* have been more concerned about the fact it was daylight, but it felt so good to stretch my wings out and swoop across the city, straight for Tyson's place.

Straight for my Evie.

Heidi had said his office was on the top floor, so I landed on the roof of Tyson's apartment building. I could've taken the window out, but there was a shred of control left within me that reminded me I could hurt Evie that way. There was no way of knowing where she'd be in the room, and barreling through a glass window gave me little control over who got hurt.

The doors on the roof were kept locked for obvious reasons, only opening from the inside.

This posed no problem.

Folding my wings away, I forced the doorhandle downward until it broke off, the lock mechanism falling noisily to the concrete in pieces. When I wrenched the door open, I heard the creak of the hinges as they protested and bent. Then using one hand, I lunged over the railing and dropped to the floor below.

Straightening, I moved silently to the door, pressing my ear against the wood and keeping low so as not to be seen, just in case anyone had heard me land and was looking out of the peephole. It occurred to me they might have cameras in the hall and the apartment, but I'd worry about that later.

The sound of someone being struck was clear through the door, followed by a whimper that I knew to be Evie. I lost what little control I had left.

There were too many people like Tyson in the world, who used others for their own gain, and people like Tyson, they were almost the worst of the worst. One step above human traffickers with just as few morals. This city had more than its fair share of people like Tyson and whoever had done what they did to Heidi and Evie.

I'd find them too.

My boot hit the door, and in my rage, I had misjudged my strength. Instead of the door slamming open, it broke in the middle, and the two halves flew into the room. Evie was tied to a chair, facing away from the door, the man I assumed to be Tyson in front of her, his hand raised to strike again, blood on his knuckles and splattered on his face.

I saw white.

I couldn't contain it.

Three steps and I was in the room, and the men to either side of the room rushed me.

But they never reached me.

My wings unfurled in all their holy glory, raised and menacing, casting an even darker shadow across my already darkened features. The men were knocked to the sides, colliding with the walls opposite. One was knocked unconscious, the other wasn't, but dared not attack me again.

Tyson's eyes widened, his hand stuck in mid-air in his shock, perpetually raised to strike again at the innocent woman in front of him. I bared my teeth and growled at him, my eyes glazing over a pure white that had the color draining from his face.

"What *are* you?" he whispered.

With a single beat of my wings, the force of which had him staggering backward from Evie and toward the window behind him, I crossed the room, my toes dragging on the carpet. I stood immediately behind Evie, bearing down on the now cowering man in front of me.

"I'm her guardian angel…" I snarled and then continued, "… and your worst nightmare."

He screamed as I grabbed the back of Evie's chair, sliding her to the side and closing the space between Tyson and me. My wings closed around me, circling him, so all he could see was my face and the shades of my wings.

He surprised me, still having some fight in him.

With a flick of his wrist, he snatched out a concealed blade and stabbed it into my shoulder. I stared at the blade for a moment in shock he had dared attack. I supposed one didn't get into his position unless they had a certain amount of bravery.

But a man like him, deep down, was filled with only cowardice.

He whimpered when I slid the blade from my shoulder, ignoring the stream of blood that followed it. That would heal itself. He cried out when I returned the gesture, stabbing the blade into his shoulder in the same spot he had mine.

He didn't deal with the pain quite as well.

I took a step back as he dropped to the floor, howling and grabbing at his shoulder.

It seemed a bit of an overreaction, but okay.

The sound of a chair being broken over my wings roused me more than any feeling I got from it. My wings were made of tougher stuff than my skin and were not easily damaged. Tyson's man backed away as I turned and advanced on him. He clutched at the broken pieces of the chair legs and held them in front of him in a cross formation with trembling hands.

I couldn't help it, I laughed.

He eyed my wings, the white of my eyes, and then glanced at the cross before dropping the wood and holding his hands up in surrender. A moment later, he fell to his knees, pressing his hands together under his chin and staring at me desperately.

"Please," he whispered. "Have mercy."

"Tell me…" I stared down at him as I wasn't going to get down to his level. "What are you willing to do to live?"

"Anything, anything. Please, don't kill me."

I pressed my hand to his forehead, and he closed his eyes, tears streaming down his face. He wasn't as dark as Tyson inside, but he was far from pure. I doubted he'd reform of his own goodwill, but I guess being a better man out of fear of the consequences was better than not trying at all. I grabbed the front of his t-shirt and dragged him to his feet, lifting until he was balancing on his toes.

This isn't how I'd normally have dealt with people like this.

But Evie, she released the animal within me.

"I'll be watching all the time. Everywhere you go, everything you do. When I let you go, you leave this building, you leave this city, and you find some way to live your life to help others." He whimpered again when I slid my hand until it was gripping his throat. "For if you don't, I *will* find you."

He nodded as best he could against my grip, and after I dropped him to the floor, he scrambled to his feet, doing a few awkward bows before backing out the doorway and disappearing down the stairs.

I turned back to Tyson. He was on his knees, still cradling his shoulder, his fingers wrapped around the handle of the knife. I watched him with my arms folded over my chest. He'd destroy the ligaments in his shoulder if he pulled it out—I had put it in on an angle.

Evidently he didn't know that, and when he tugged it from his shoulder, he cried out in pain again, a pathetic broken shout ending in a sob.

I almost laughed again.

Then I realized another human trait had rubbed off on me. An undesirable trait I should've known better than to let it get the best of me.

Arrogance.

I was so sure I had the upper hand that when Tyson stumbled to his feet and lunged for Evie, I was too slow to react, too busy enjoying the moment of him destroying the use of one of his arms.

But he only needed one arm to hold the knife to her throat.

"Back the fuck off, man, or I'll bleed her out in front of you."

Evie was watching me, her face bruised and blood dripping from her lips, but he hadn't cut her. Her eyes were glazed. I wondered how much she'd had to drink and if it had helped numb the pain he had put her through.

But then I realized that while I could smell the alcohol, the glaze of her eyes wasn't because she was tipsy or drunk.

They were tears.

Her eyes were on mine, and although I'm sure she had taken in my appearance, me as I am, wings and all, all she was doing was watching my eyes. I felt them slide back into blue as I looked at her, and it was only then tears shifted from a glaze to falling down her cheeks in steady streams. Perhaps she recognized the man beyond the angel, the man she had been with, made love with, and ran her nails down his back.

The woman I needed and wanted and would protect forevermore never stopped looking at my eyes.

She didn't seem panicked, and for that, I was thankful.

She trusted me to save her.

CHAPTER
23

EVIE

When I saw him, I didn't even feel the tip of the blade Tyson held against my throat push into my skin.

Zaqiel.

He was glorious.

That body, those eyes, those *wings.*

Angels don't do this, he had said.

How on Earth was I supposed to know he meant it literally?

That he wasn't comparing himself to me, putting himself on some angelic pedestal compared to the scum that was my existence.

How was I to know?

It all made sense—his hesitation and how he punished himself for being with me.

Hell, if angels could be imperfect, then I didn't

feel so bad.

His wings were magnificent, spanning almost the entire reach of the apartment, a display of steel and lighter grays, all flowing together and creating a wall of power around him. I felt the tears come when his eyes shifted from the supernatural white back to his blue, and I couldn't stop looking at him. All I wanted to do was to touch him, to have him wrap me up in his arms and take me away from this place.

He had come for me.

That was huge.

I didn't know how he knew where I was and if he had been watching me this entire time, but that did not matter. Because just when I felt a spark of hope inside me, a will to live, to keep going, there he was. He was my salvation, and I wanted to be his.

"Zaqiel," I whispered, my lip trembling.

Tyson pushed the blade harder against my neck. He had reached out to get the blade near me before Zaqiel could react, and since then, he had moved behind me. His breathing was ragged and heavy against my ear and shoulder, and I hated him being this close. I don't think I've ever hated anyone as much as I hated Tyson right now, and that was saying something. It burned through me like a white-hot rage, and I clenched my fingers over the arms of the chair.

"Is this the fucker who took you away?" Tyson

almost laughed. "Well, fuck me, Evie, you sure do keep some interesting company."

When Zaqiel told him to drop the knife, his voice dark and foreboding, I was surprised Tyson had the gall to press it harder against my throat, drawing blood that trickled down my neck and chest.

"Drop the knife, Tyson," Zaqiel demanded.

"Get fucked, you freak. If I can't have her, no one can."

Zaqiel met my eyes before they slid to Tyson behind me, and I saw something in them, something that I'd be afraid of if it were directed at me.

He moved so fast he was simply a blur of gray as he shot toward me. I screamed as the knife was dragged across my throat, not deep enough to kill, but perhaps would be another scar to add, before the knife was dropped uselessly to the floor. Ducking my head, I cowered as the window next to me shattered in an explosion of sound.

Then there was silence, and I was left in the room, empty save for one of Tyson's still unconscious goons in the corner. Frantically, I searched outside for any sign of Zaqiel, but he was gone, Tyson as well.

Working my hands against the ropes, I was still unable to get any give from the binds. Eyeing the knife on the floor, I started to rock the chair to the sides until it tipped over. I was ready for the impact, but it didn't make it any less painful against my already bruised shoulder, and I hissed air through my teeth.

I was inches from the knife, my fingers stretching across the carpet as I tried to hop the chair closer when I heard the scream. A man's scream pitched with terror.

I froze and waited.

Nothing.

Scrambling for the knife again, I cried out when a boot landed on it.

"What are you doing?"

Zaqiel.

I hated it, but I began to cry, relief flooding through me. Not only at being saved from Tyson, but being saved from this life, being saved by this man. Deep down, I knew he wouldn't leave me again. I had seen him, everything he was, and I was his now, and he was mine.

He kneeled, grabbing the chair and lifting it back up as though it weighed nothing before taking the knife and carefully cutting through the binds. His eyes were swimming with concern when he looked at me, brushing his thumb across the thin line of blood on my throat. I shuddered under his touch.

He grinned, and I melted. "Did you really think I'd leave you tied to this chair?"

Rubbing my wrists, I shook my head, managing a small smile in return. "I don't like to wait."

He helped me to my feet. His wings were no

longer visible, and when he saw me looking for them, he tilted his head but said nothing. When I reached out to touch his shoulder, he unfolded his wings, appearing on his back and splaying out, knocking over a table.

Gasping, I reached toward him, and when he didn't stop me, I brushed my fingers delicately against the feathers. For some reason, I had expected them to be soft, but they felt stronger than I thought, offering resistance when I pushed my fingertips against them. When I took one of the feathers in between my fingers and stroked it, he hummed, and I watched as his eyes closed. I smirked—he was like a damn puppy.

His eyes snapped open, and he saw my grin, the corner of his lip lifting in that almost smile he does. Sharply, I withdrew my hand when he folded his wings up again, no sign of them on this back as if they never existed.

He lifted me under my knees and shoulders and cradled me against his chest, stepping on the broken pieces of the door as he left the apartment.

I sighed into his chest. "I knew you'd come for me."

He chuckled, a deep rumbling against my ear. "Liar."

CHAPTER
24

EVIE

He carried me to my apartment. I didn't argue about being carried but simply wrapped my arms around his neck and allowed it. There was strength in this, the submission in letting myself be cared for and protected. I can't remember the last time someone had tried to protect me but nuzzling into his neck and feeling the deep rumble of his chuckle, it didn't matter. Because I had Zaqiel now.

God, when had I turned into such a sap?

Zaqiel stopped abruptly, and I looked up. We weren't quite at my building, and he was staring at a man trying to get in, one hand banging on the locked door and the other with his phone pressed to his ear.

I gasped, and Zaqiel pulled me closer to his chest.

"Who are you?" Zaqiel called, not even a hint of a smile on his face but the same dark, blank expression he had held for so long. Seemingly indifferent, but I knew now, absorbing everything that happened, he cared much more than he admitted.

The man looked up, relief flooding his face. I patted Zaqiel on the shoulder to let me down, but he simply pulled me closer to him, his large arms folding around me and keeping me close to him.

"Evie!" The man rushed toward us as fast as he could manage but stopped when Zaqiel took a step back, the darkness creeping across his face.

"It's okay, Zaqiel. He's a friend."

He looked down at me and hesitated for a long moment before lowering me to the ground, grasping my elbow when I stumbled before keeping his arm protectively around my waist. Clive took my hands, and I swear I heard Zaqiel growl.

"Are you okay?"

"I'm so sorry I scared you, Clive. I forgot I had called."

"You called him?"

Looking at Zaqiel as he spoke, I couldn't help the lift of my lip as I almost laughed as possessive rage flashed across his face. "I had no one else to call, Zaqiel. I was alone and scared." I turned back to Clive. "And drunk. I'm so sorry I wasted your time."

He eyed my neck, no doubt taking in the blood

before his eyes traced over the angry red marks on my arms and shoulders and the bruises that would be forming on my face. Self-consciously, I licked my lips and felt the dry blood with my tongue. I must look a mess.

"You didn't waste my time. It looks like you needed help." He glanced at Zaqiel, who didn't relax even after the friendly smile Clive offered him. "But thank God this young man was here to save you."

"Yes." I grinned. "*Thank God.*"

Clive took my hands again. "I take it this means we won't be seeing each other again?"

"I'm afraid not, but—"

"Evie," Zaqiel interrupted me, his voice still stony. "Do you trust this man?"

I looked back at Clive, his eyes so full of kindness. "Yes, yes, I think I do."

"Heidi," he said simply.

I whirled around and asked, "You found her? Is she okay?"

His face looked pained, and I felt my heart drop in my chest. "Not exactly."

I understood. He didn't need to say anything further. "Where is she?"

"At my place."

"Clive, may I give your number to a friend of mine? When she's ready, I think she may need some company."

"Does she work with you?" He looked

uncomfortable, shooting an embarrassed look at Zaqiel.

"No." I tried to keep my smile reassuring. "I just think she'd like to meet you."

Zaqiel had insisted he carry me to my apartment and then further insisted I drink a glass of water. But slowly, *slowly.* He scolded me as though I couldn't look after myself, with a constant frown plastered on his face as he watched me drink.

"Do you want a shower?" he asked.

"Are you offering to join me?"

His eyes shot to mine, having been watching my hands as he ran his thumbs across the inside of my palms. His eyebrow cocked, and there was a spark to his eyes that was instantly replaced with concern.

"Evie..."

I laughed. "Relax, will you? You can wash my back."

"You've been through a lot, and I don't feel you're coping with this grief."

Taking his face in my hands, I planted a kiss on his lips that left his eyes darting between mine. "I'm not an idiot, Zaqiel. A lot of fucked-up shit has happened. I'll deal with it, but later. Right now, I just want to enjoy this moment with you."

"Because you're scared it won't last?"

The smile fell from my lips. *How did he know that's what I was thinking?* "I—"

He grabbed my wrists and gripped, almost painfully. "I mean what I said before. I'm sorry I hurt you, but I'll *not* leave you again."

I allowed myself a small smile, kissed him again, and stood to make my way to the bathroom. He was immediately behind me, his hands hovering around my waist, ready to catch me if I swayed or fell. His proximity was reassuring, although I still grabbed onto the towel rack out of instinct rather than falling against him, not used to having his presence so close to protect me.

I chuckled to myself because I'm sure, in no time at all, I'd be so used to his presence I wouldn't want to live without him.

The childish part of me wanted to stumble, to feel how quickly he could move, how fast his hands would grab me and hold me again to make sure I was okay. I got the feeling he wasn't going to let me out of his sight ever again, that he'd spend every day making up for everything, and I would too. I also realized if I wanted to touch him and be touched by him, I didn't have to pretend to fall. I could simply turn around and touch him because he'd be right there.

So, I let myself feel safe with him. I let the guard down and realized I'd have to try to remember who I was beyond it.

He slid a steadying arm around my waist as he reached past me to turn the shower on, lightly swatting my hands when I went to remove my clothes, I obediently lifted my arms so he could slide my top off. When I flinched with the exertion to my shoulder, he frowned again. Kneeling in front of me, he slid my pants down, tapping the inside of my ankles until I stepped out of them as I rested my hands on his head to balance myself. As he stood, the vulnerability surged in me. Here I was, naked in front of this man, who beyond the fact that physically he was an imposing figure—tall and sculpted— he was an angel.

A literal fucking angel.

Should I be panicking or freaking out? Should I be questioning my place in this world, my mortality, and what exists beyond this Earth? But all I could do was focus on his eyes and know that I knew the man beyond the supernatural. I could deal with the rest later.

The strength I noticed when we first met, I imagined it was only part of what he was capable of.

I wondered if he was strong enough to hold me up and fuck me as he hovered above the city, those big, beautiful wings of his beating against the wind.

He could kill me in an instant or hurt me by accident even.

There was strength in the vulnerability, I think, in allowing myself to be vulnerable with him, letting him see the part of me that had been peeking through my inner darkness with increasing insistence since we met. It was as though, because my whole life I had been hiding behind a mask of false bravado and indifference, now that I was exposed as only human, it was too much.

Invigorating but too much.

I trembled slightly as he touched my shoulders, and he rubbed his thumbs across my skin before lifting my chin with his fingers. That concern was still written on his face. I imagined it was an emotion he usually didn't allow himself to show, and I was honored he was willing to show it with me.

"Are you going to get naked too?" I asked, very aware of my nudity as I took him in, still in cargo pants, boots, and a t-shirt.

"Later. Let me wash you now."

Nodding, I took his hand as I stepped over the edge of the bathtub and under the warm flow of the shower, lifting my face into the water and allowing it to wash away the day. But more than that, allowing it to wash away the months and years, and every moment up until now because none of those moments mattered anymore.

Although I realized as I looked at my arms, I'd always have the reminders of those years.

Zaqiel lathered up his hands with soap, and with a touch that was almost unbelievably gentle, he began to wash my back, working his fingers delicately into my shoulders to rub out the knots but not aggravate the bruises. When he traced his fingers down my back, I shivered and turned my head just enough to see that half-smile of his. He kept pushing that button, tracing my scars over and over every time we met, perhaps knowing that one day I'd let him do it.

But I could turn the tables on him. He may be an angel, but I knew how to press his buttons too.

Facing him, I reached forward and grabbed his cock through his pants, smirking when I could feel he was already hard.

He looked embarrassed for a moment before that dark expression took over.

"Let me guess..." I whispered, *"Angels aren't supposed to do this?"*

His eyes flashed dangerously as his gaze traced my body.

"There are a lot of things we're not supposed to do."

I squealed as he stepped over the edge of the bath, still fully clothed, and I flinched as my back was pressed against the cold tiles as he advanced on me, pinning me between his hard chest and the wall. His mouth was on mine in an instant, the water trickling down our hair and necks and over our cheeks, meeting where our lips met and sending my mind conflicting sensations of hot and cold.

"Zaqiel!" I cried as his hands found my thighs, hitching one leg up and draping it over his waist, grinding his erection against my warmth, the rough fabric of his pants only adding another level of sensation. "God!" I gasped.

He grunted, rutting against me as my hands scrambled against his back, and I bit into his shoulder. His clothes were soaked, but he didn't seem to care, and neither did I.

But I did care that he was wearing too many of them.

He got the hint when I started yanking at his shirt and pulled it over his head, dropping it into the bathtub with a wet thud that splashed my ankles with cool water.

"Don't you want to go to the bedroom?" I panted.

He was undoing his pants, letting them drop to his ankles. With another kiss, he grabbed my face with one hand, forcing me to look away from his erect cock and into his eyes. "No," he growled. "Is that a problem?"

I shook my head as he lifted me under my thighs and ass, pressing my back hard against the wall as he penetrated me. Crying out, I tilted my head back against the wall, stretching my neck with my mouth hanging open in silent prayer. He was so big, stretching and forcing me to accommodate his length and girth every time.

Promising to be this good forevermore.

He wasn't going to last long, not this time, not after all the anger and emotions had built up to this. I could tell by his uneven breathing, his breath hot against my collarbone, and how he missed a beat with his thrusts every now and then. That's okay because I wasn't going to last long either. He was so close and hitting all the best angles, I could feel my pleasure building as my pussy further slickened with arousal with every one of his thrusts.

When he came, his fingers tensed against my flesh, and I bit into his shoulder to cover the cry that escaped my lips. He continued rutting against me, his growls lost against my skin before he slowly pulled out, resting his head against the cold tiles with me sandwiched between his body and the wall.

"Heaven on Earth," he mumbled.

And I don't think I've ever felt purer.

CHAPTER 25

ZAQIEL

Taking my time, I finished washing her, taking extra care because although she didn't say anything, it was a pang in my chest to know I may have aggravated her injuries when I took her in the shower. But I couldn't help it. I needed her before, but this time it was different. I knew I wouldn't have even made it to the bedroom. Evie was mine now. I shouldn't have let her go before, and I wasn't ever going to again. The need to claim her, to own her, to penetrate her, consumed me.

She watched me with her eyebrow arched while I towel-dried her. I knew I was being possessive, and thankfully I had gotten to her in time before Tyson did any major damage. Apart from the shock of the situation and a few minor injuries and aches, she was quite capable of drying herself.

But I liked touching her, so I arched an eyebrow at her in response, silently asking her if she had a problem with me taking care of her. The small smirk I got in return told me she didn't, but she was still going to give me a hard time about it.

When I smiled at her, her eyes lit up.

Wrapping the towel around her, I helped her stand and followed Evie to the bed, sitting next to her. When she sank to her knees on the ground, I grabbed at her shoulders.

"Evie, are you okay?"

Had the shock caught up with her? Was she passing out?

"Shh, Zaqiel, I'm fine."

I didn't let go of her shoulders as she kneeled in front of me and finished undoing my belt, which I had only partially done up after I had taken her in the shower. I said her name over and over again as she tugged down my still-soaked pants and wrapped them into a ball, tossing them into the bathroom.

"You shouldn't sit in wet clothes, you'll catch a chill."

"Evie, please, you don't have to."

As she ran her fingernails up my thighs, I groaned. "That's just the thing, Zaqiel. I don't *have* to, but I want to."

I was hard again already, and I looked away. My very human response to her was still something I was getting used to not being embarrassed about. I loved that she made me feel this way, that my body responded to her when my mind was still reeling with feelings I didn't yet understand.

"But you're hurt. He hit you, your jaw—"

My words were cut off when she wrapped her fingers around my length. "Zaqiel, please. Can you just let me? I want to please you."

"Evie—" I gasped when she took me in her mouth, working her tongue around. *"Fuck,"* I hissed through gritted teeth, earning a cheeky smile from her as her lips hovered over my erect length. Gripping the mattress between my fingers, she worked her mouth and hand in tandem up and down my length. I tried to resist the urge to buck my hips from the edge of the bed into her mouth, but I couldn't stop. Her mouth was so warm and welcoming around me, but she used her hands to stop me from going too deep, for which I was grateful. I didn't want to choke her.

I felt the mattress protest and groan under my grip before it ripped.

Lifting her head from my lap, she gasped at the damage.

"Guess there goes my deposit for this place."

"I'm sorry." I hastily lifted my hands from the mattress.

"I'm joking, Zaqiel. I don't care."

I went to answer but forgot the words as she

took me in her mouth again. This time I couldn't stop myself. I placed my hands on her head, twisting my fingers into her damp hair and thrusting my hips up, so I went deeper. I hesitated, and when she looked up at me, she gave me the slightest nod, and I smiled. Holding her head still, I thrust into her throat, groaning loudly as she took me, flicking her tongue around the head and letting me claim her. Feeling my climax building, I relinquished control to her, letting her work me until I was moaning and came into her mouth.

Panting, I watched her with wide eyes as she released me and licked from the base to the tip of my cock, a cheeky grin adorning her face.

"Evie, my God…"

I twitched when she kissed the tip before she climbed onto the bed, pushing me down with a palm to my chest and lying next to me, snuggled against my side.

She fit next to me so perfectly.

Evie had fallen asleep for a while, and I had let her rest, stroking her shoulder in small circles with my fingertips and listening to the steady sound of her breathing. She was so relaxed, and I hoped that meant she understood she was safe now.

It was early evening when she woke, shifting and mumbling against me. I kissed the top of her head, and sleepily, she kissed my chest.

"What happened to Tyson?" she asked.

She was drowsy, still half-asleep. The past few days and weeks had taken their toll, and she was struggling to come into the world of the waking. I wanted her to rest, so why must she ask such difficult questions?

"Go back to sleep, Evie."

My refusal to answer her question had the opposite effect than I had been hoping, and she shifted again, resting her chin on my chest and looking at me earnestly. "What happened to Tyson?" When I didn't answer but continued to stare at the ceiling, she said, "I need to know if he's going to come after me or Heidi again."

"He won't be coming after you."

"What happened, Zaqiel?"

I hesitated again, and her fingers gripped where her hand rested on my chest. "He jumped, Evie, he jumped."

She was silent for a long moment. "Are you telling me the truth?"

I let my gaze slowly move from the dirty ceiling to her eyes. "I'm not lying to you. I can't go around killing humans, Evie. I'd be stripped of my wings."

"Why did he jump?"

I stared at the ceiling again. "He was afraid of me."

She looked at me for a while longer before shifting again and resting her head in the crook of my arm. After a while, I felt her breathing slow. She wasn't quite sleeping, only snoozing, but in a state of relaxation again.

I didn't lie to her. Tyson had jumped from the roof.

I had flown him from the apartment onto the roof and may have dropped him from higher than necessary when I let him down. With my eyes blazing white and my wings spread out, he had backed away from me as fast as he could. I had offered him an ultimatum, much like I had with one of his goons who had broken a chair over my back. But Tyson was full of much more darkness than that man was, darkness and stubbornness that ran deep within him. He had laughed it off, a maniacal laugh that edged on insanity, not an uncommon reaction people had at being faced with the truth of celestial beings.

He called me on my lie, claiming I couldn't possibly be watching him all the time, and if he left the city, I had no way of knowing if he continued somewhere else doing what he was doing here.

He was right.

I saw him glancing over the edge of the building,

calculating his chances. I told him what the chances were of his survival.

I guess he liked those odds, but that didn't bode well for him.

I think I should've felt worse than I did.

But looking at Evie, I was simply thankful for her safety.

CHAPTER
26

EVIE

Squeezing her close to me, I ignored her indignant noises at the overt display of affection.

"Heidi, I'm so sorry I couldn't protect you."

"It's not up to you to protect me," she mumbled against my shoulder. "You did what you could."

Leaning back, I took her shoulders in my hands and surveyed her face. When she went to hold a hand up to her cheek and turn away, I grabbed her wrist, waiting until she looked back at me, dying inside at the tears that streamed down her face.

"Everything will be okay now," I said.

She eyed Zaqiel over my shoulder. "For you, maybe."

"For you too." I shook her shoulders until she looked at me again. "For you too," I repeated. Her eyes flooded with tears, but she nodded. I could tell she didn't believe me, but she wanted to. I rubbed my thumb along the edge of her scar. Once the stitches were out and she was more healed, I'd ask her if she wanted to meet Clive.

It would be up to her after all. Even if they only stayed in touch for a short while, just long enough to show her she's worth much more than she thinks she is, can do anything she wants, and doesn't need to live this life.

Things I already knew and wish I had the power to do something about before. Maybe I did have the power, maybe I simply needed to be shown what was on the other side of the darkness. But playing around with *what-ifs* wasn't going to help me now.

For the first time in a long time, I needed to focus on moving forward.

With Tyson out of the picture, there'd be a power struggle amongst his remaining employees. I didn't doubt someone would take his place, and there was every chance they would be as dark as he was. But by then, the girls would've scattered. Zaqiel had already expressed thoughts to me about showing them how to look after themselves. If they wanted to continue working, they could, but they didn't need a *manager*. They could do it without a solitary character controlling their finances. Zaqiel had made friends with his landlord in the time he had been there and was sure he wouldn't mind his building being full and receiving rent. He didn't seem the type to judge the girls, and he might even be able to offer them a level of security.

Obviously, I wouldn't go back to working, but I had no idea what I would do now. Perhaps I could be a waitress or a hostess at a fancy restaurant.

Maybe Clive knew someone.

I didn't want to push my luck asking Clive for favors, but if I had learned anything, it was that there were times when you needed to reach out and ask for help.

And not everyone wanted to hurt me.

Heidi lived with Zaqiel and me in his apartment for a few weeks. During this time, Zaqiel made arrangements with his landlord regarding the rest of the girls to get them to safety before Tyson's goons figured out what had happened and who would take over. Tyson's entire business had collapsed quickly, and although there were many others around like it, there was good done in the world because of this.

Good which I had to constantly remind Zaqiel of because it seemed no matter how many people he helped and what difference he made in the lives of others, it was never enough for him.

So as I sat cross-legged on our bed, cradling a glass of white wine, I watched while he stared out the window.

"You've done so much good, Zaqiel," I said to his back. "You can rest for a while."

"There are always people who need help, Evie," he mumbled. "It's not enough."

"It's more than enough." I set the wine down on the bedside table and stood next to him, looking out across the city. "You're giving so much of yourself to this city, it's killing you."

Wrapping an arm around my waist, he pulled me against him. I looked up, and there was that almost smile I had grown to love. It made his proper smiles all the more special. "It won't kill me."

I slapped the ball of my palm into my forehead in an exaggerated manner. "Sorry, forgot you were an *angel*."

There was the twitch of the corner of his mouth again. "Must you say it like that?"

"Like what?"

"*Angel,* like you're one step away from holding up your fingers and making air quotes. I'm an angel. Pure and simple."

I chuckled and nodded against his chest as I leaned into him. "Pure and simple."

Turning as there was a knock on the bedroom door, I called Heidi in. She had her stitches removed earlier today and had a gauze pad covering half of her face.

"I thought of something," Heidi said. I watched as she twisted her hands together and waited for her to speak again. "What about Paul?" she whispered.

My heart sank, and Zaqiel's brows pulled together as he felt me stiffen next to him. "Who's Paul?" he asked.

I hesitated, but I could already feel Zaqiel tensing as if he already knew what the answer was. Heidi must have seen something in his eyes, for her own grew wide before she glanced away, looking at me instead while she answered the question.

"He's the one who gave me this scar and who almost killed Evie."

A deep growl emanated from Zaqiel, rumbling through his chest. "Give me his name." He forced the words out through gritted teeth. I placed my palms flat on his chest as though I could force him to calm through will alone. I don't know how Heidi would react if he lost control and unfurled his wings. As Heidi told Zaqiel Paul's full name, he stilled, thinking.

"Zaqiel, please don't do anything stupid," I said.

I wasn't sure he had heard me, and when he looked down at me after a long pause, I saw the white flash across his eyes, even as his lips curled into a dark smile.

“Evie, when have you ever known me to do something stupid?”

CHAPTER
27

EVIE

Before Heidi had moved out, she had agreed to meet with Clive. She returned from their dinner date gushing like a schoolgirl, and unlike me, she had allowed him to walk her home. Except they hadn't walked, he had driven her, and while part of me expected a red sports car, he instead drove a practical black sedan that screamed class.

Heidi moved into a different apartment in the same building as us, and Zaqiel stood in the hall with his arms crossed, surveying her new neighbors as I helped her unpack her clothes.

Protective and possessive—sides of him he hadn't let out before.

And I liked it.

But he wasn't yet fully out of his shell and didn't want to have sex while Heidi was in our apartment—he felt it was disrespectful. So, our naked time, which I felt was nowhere near enough, had been limited to when she was out.

But judging by the way he was staring at me from his vantage point in the hall, the darkness that passed over his face with every move I made, I was in trouble tonight.

He was on me before we had even crossed the threshold into the apartment, backing me up against the wall as he kicked the door closed with a slam. His mouth was hungry and greedy on mine, and his hands wandered over my body, trying to touch as much of me as he could. I moaned even as I giggled against his mouth.

"What are you laughing at?" he grunted as he mouthed his way down my neck and over my collar bone, nipping at the sensitive skin.

"You," I whispered. "You're so eager."

I felt his smile against my neck as his hands found my breasts and kneaded them gently, enticing another moan from me.

"Is that a problem?"

"Not at all."

I grabbed the back of his neck and pulled him to me, pushing my tongue into his mouth before moaning again and letting him dominate the kiss.

There was an annoying sound in the background, but I was almost too lost in the pleasure to notice it. But it stopped and started again three times. I wrenched myself away from Zaqiel.

"Someone's calling me."

"Leave it."

"They keep calling, Zaqiel. It might be important."

With a heavy sigh, he dropped his hands to his sides, shoving them in his pockets and looking as though he was on the border of a pout as I crossed the room and answered the phone.

The voice on the other end was frantic and whispering, and I had to take the phone away from my ear and check the caller identification before I could place the voice.

"Alexis? What's wrong? What's going on?"

Zaqiel's face had changed as his posture straightened, and he crossed the room to me, pausing before speaking when I held a finger up in front of him. Alexis was whispering, every other word cut out as she sobbed

"Just stay there. Just keep quiet and stay there. We're on our way."

"What is it?" Zaqiel asked the moment I hung up.

"Someone's tearing up the bar... the Union." I

twisted my hands together as the full intensity of the situation settled over my shoulders. "He's holding all the girls there and has a gun."

CHAPTER
28

ZAQIEL

Short of tying Evie to the bed, which I'll admit was quite tempting, there was nothing I could do to stop her from coming with me to the Union. The girls she had worked with for months, cared for them when they got hurt, and had stayed at their homes when she didn't feel safe in hers were there and needed help.

Although she told me she never slept well when she was in someone else's home, it was nice having the presence there, a body in the other room she could wake if there was danger, but she never really slept.

Couldn't trust anyone fully.

To save time, Evie consented to let me fly us there, and despite the seriousness of the situation we were heading toward, I could tell she was lost in the moment of flight. The cool evening air whipped her hair around her face, and she wanted to smile. I could see the way her eyes lit up. But she couldn't let herself enjoy this moment, her arms clutched around my neck with her hands instinctively flexing and relaxing. She wasn't afraid that I'd drop her, she was scared for the girls.

I landed us around the corner from the bar, grabbing Evie's arm when she moved to run onto the street.

"Stay behind me," I said.

"But—"

"Stay. Behind. Me."

She stared at me defiantly for a moment longer before she nodded, and I took my time relaxing my grip on her arm. But she was true to her agreement and didn't bolt despite the way she fidgeted with an eagerness to jump into the situation, her own safety forgotten in lieu of others. Instead, she allowed me to lead the way onto the street and around the front of the bar after folding my wings away.

At Evie's insistence, I entered the bar with my hands raised, keeping her behind me.

A warning shot rang out, hitting the doorframe next to my head.

"We're just here to talk!" Evie called out over my shoulder. "We're unarmed."

I took in the scene. There were at least a dozen girls and almost as many bar-goers around, lying down with their hands on the back of their heads and faces to the floor. I wondered how Evie's friend had managed to call her without the shooter seeing.

But then I saw him, and I understood.

"Lee?" Evie said. "What are you doing?"

I knew that man, although I didn't know his name until now. He was the man I had let go when I had rescued Evie, an employee of Tyson's who I had felt there was enough good left in him to start a new life and do something better. Apparently, I had judged him wrong, along with many other humans I had misjudged over the years.

He didn't look good.

Not that he looked particularly good before, although I may have had a skewed vision of him and judged him by his involvement in Evie's kidnap and abuse. Evil deeds tended to warp someone's physical appearance. Someone could be attractive, then when you saw their true colors, suddenly they were not.

Like Candy.

Whether Lee was actively involved in Tyson's acts or not, he stood by while Evie and others were treated as they were and did nothing.

Now, his eyes held that manic look of someone on the edge, and his hand that held the gun now pointed at my chest, was trembling. His clothes were filthy as though he hadn't washed in days or weeks, and his hair was unkempt.

He looked unbalanced.

"You!" He managed to push out through gritted teeth. "I knew you would come if they called Evie, *guardian angel.*"

"What do you want?"

"You, I want you."

The rage was bubbling inside me again, a feeling I was becoming all too familiar with now. Something I had been able to keep mostly under control until I had someone to care for, something to lose.

"You did *all* of this..." I indicated to his hostages cowering on the ground, "... just to get to me?"

He laughed a maniacal, unsettling sound that reaffirmed my suspicions he was on the edge.

"Ooh," he cooed. "You were bound to come running, weren't you? Come flying in to protect these whores, just like you did Evie."

"What do you want?"

"You *fucked me up,* dude! How am I supposed to know what to do with myself now that I know what I know? Now that I know you exist?"

"Do what I told you to do... *help people.*"

He laughed again. "Fuck that for a joke. I'll sleep better at night if you aren't around."

I let my expression darken, tilting my head down and allowing the white to take over my eyes. "I don't want you to sleep better at night."

"Zaqiel..." Evie whispered, the urgency clear in

her voice. "We need to get him out of here. He could hurt someone."

She was right, of course.

"Lee," I started, noticing his unpleasant expression when I used his name. I pulled a face too. I didn't like talking to him any more than he liked being talked to by me. "Why don't we take this outside?"

"I ain't going anywhere with you without some collateral."

He searched around and was about to reach down and grab one of the girls when Evie screamed, "Stop!"

Lee stared at her, his hand stretched and inches from the top of the head of the girl nearest him, who had begun to tremble visibly.

"Take me."

"Evie, no. What are you doing?" She wrenched against the grip I took on her arm, but I wouldn't let her go.

I couldn't let her go.

"Zaqiel…" she whispered. "I have to help them. *We* have to help them."

Lee was crossing the bar, stepping over the bodies of his hostages still lying face down on the ground. He stopped two feet away at the look he got from me.

They had heard it.

"The cops are coming," I said to Lee. "We better

get out of here before this gets real messy."

"You going to kill me, winged freak?"

"I'm not going to kill you."

He stared at me for a beat longer, and I took an experimental step backward. He didn't react. Stretching an arm protectively over Evie, who had made herself visible to him so he wouldn't take one of the others, I watched his hand carefully as the gun he held was now pointed at her, straight at what he could see of her beyond my shoulder and arm. Lee didn't need to know much about me to know that I wouldn't risk her. So, slowly and carefully, we left the bar.

The slow pace we had left the bar with increased as the sound of the sirens got closer. I doubted Lee wanted to deal with the police any more than I did. He was willing to move as long as he could see a snippet of Evie and could keep his gun trained on her. I tried to keep her hidden with my body in such a way that meant I could protect her if Lee were to shoot, but there was that nagging sense of doubt in me I wouldn't be able to move fast enough to stop a bullet, and she could get hurt.

This, and this alone, is what kept me compliant and not tearing Lee limb from limb.

The first alley we came across, he guided us into with a flick of his wrist. Once hidden mostly from the street's view, I turned to face Lee, hiding Evie behind me.

"What do you want?" I asked again.

He had started to shake more now, a motion that had begun in his hand until his entire body was visibly trembling. I'd have had more sympathy for the man if it weren't for what I knew of his past, had given him a chance at a fresh start, and that he had thrown it away.

No one is a lost cause.

Do you really believe that?

He had held up a bar of mostly innocent people, turning them into hostages, and for what? Because he was having some existential crisis and inner conflict over the new knowledge of celestial beings? I get it, it was a lot to take in, but I didn't see Evie going crazy with that manic look in her eyes, threatening to hurt people. So, my patience was limited to none with this man.

"I told you, I can't sleep knowing you're out there."

"Well, I don't know what you expect me to do about—"

I stopped when he withdrew the items from his pocket.

It seems like he *had* been busy over these past few weeks.

"Zaqiel, what is it?"

"Stay behind me, Evie."

"Zaqiel—"

I pushed her further behind me and tried to ignore the panic that had been in her voice. She didn't know what it was that Lee held in his hands, but she must have sensed the tenseness in my shoulders, the way my back straightened and breath hitched.

Yeah, he had been a busy man.

Doing his research, gathering information.

I don't think I've ever misjudged a man as much as I did this one. He knew the gun meant nothing to me, that the only reason I feared it was because of the damage it could do to Evie, and he couldn't kill me with metal or bullets.

But burning holy oil, that was something else entirely.

And the bottle and lighter he held told me he meant business.

If all I could get out of this was making sure Evie

was safe, then I could be happy with that. Because Lee meant business, and it was like cutting a razor over my heart to know this was because I had given someone a second chance. I had found Evie, found heaven on Earth, found happiness, and things I didn't even know I was capable of feeling, and because I had tried to see the best in someone, I may lose it all.

Irony. It wasn't the least bit amusing.

"Lee," I held my hands out in front of me. "Put those down, you don't know what you're doing."

"I know *exactly* what I'm doing. How many times do I have to keep telling you? I can't sleep knowing you're around. What is your kind doing on Earth anyway? We've been fine without you."

I almost laughed. "You have no idea what you're talking about. We've always been around."

"Well, you can fuck off because we don't need you." He flicked the lighter and noticed I flinched, which brought a smile to his face. "This world is hard enough to make it in as it is with fucked-up humans, I don't need supernatural bullshit to deal with too."

"Lee, you're being ridiculous." Evie struggled against my hold. I couldn't hold her and stop him at the same time, and she was my priority. I twisted around to hold her back from coming in front of me, trying to act as a human shield against something she didn't understand.

"Let me go, Zaqiel," she hissed.

"Evie, *please*, I have to protect you."

Lee was faster than I gave him credit for and more cowardly for attacking when my back was turned. I had only enough time to push Evie away from me before the oil he had thrown on my back was ignited by the lighter.

CHAPTER
29

EVIE

"Zaqiel!"

I've never heard that sound before—a scream so pitched with terror that it grated against your skin and sent a trail of goosebumps springing up on your arms.

It took me a moment to realize the scream had come from me.

Zaqiel shoved me away from him only a split second before he went up in flames. They engulfed his back and arms and sent me reeling at the instant heat. Almost unnatural flames of overly bright yellows and oranges licked at his skin and crept around his shoulders and torso, disintegrating his shirt and eating away at his skin.

"No!" I screamed again and reached out for him as he stumbled away from me. I suspected the pain in his eyes wasn't entirely due to the way his skin was growing red then black and blistering under the flames.

I heard the beginnings of a laugh, a few short notes before it grew frantic.

"What did you *do,* Lee?" I cried.

The laughing stopped, his eyes turned to me, and I shrunk under his gaze. He radiated a madness, danger, and general misbalance that crossed the air between us and filled me with discomfort that made me tremble.

"How does one woman know an angel, I wonder?" he said, tapping himself on the chin with the lighter. "Unless she, too, is one of these supernatural beings."

"Lee—"

"You're next, bitch," he cried.

The roar that came from Zaqiel set me on edge, and when he turned on Lee, I had to move back a few feet from the heat radiating from the flames on his back.

"Stay away from her!" he cried, and although I reached out to him and called his name, I don't think he heard me. What could I have even done anyway? I could feel Zaqiel's pain from his movements, the way he held himself, but somehow, he still found the strength to grab Lee by the throat and hurled him out of the alleyway and onto the street.

The timing was either perfect or really bad, depending on how you wanted to look at it because as Lee flew across the street in an arc, he was collected by a passing car before he even hit the ground.

Even as the brakes were screeching, bringing the car to a halt, Zaqiel fell to his knees. I pulled my top off and wrapped it around him the best I could, extinguishing the flames and ignoring that my hands burned every time I made contact. Zaqiel had finally succumbed to the pain and was writhing and screaming in a way that shattered my heart and made it feel like it was being wrenched from my chest. His screams were unnatural, pitches and tones that beyond broke my heart as they destroyed my soul.

The burning effect was quicker on him than it was on my hands and more severe. When the flames were out, he stayed on his knees, his breaths were labored and heavy, his back and shoulders rising and falling, almost black save for the angry red blisters dotted through the burns. There was nothing left of his shirt, and his chest and lower half of his face were no better. I fell to my knees next to him, wanting to hold him but not wanting to hurt him any further. As I watched cracks appear in his skin between the burns, ash flaked away even in the slight breeze.

"Zaqiel, oh my God, what can I do?"

He was no longer screaming, but the labored rasps of his breathing and the silence were almost as disturbing.

"Evie…"

"I'm here, Zaqiel." I choked back a sob, wanting to be strong for him when he needed me, but all I could see was the man I loved being taken away from me much too soon before we'd even had a chance to have a real life together.

"I'm sorry," he coughed. "I never meant to hurt you."

"I don't care about that, Zaqiel. I don't care about any of that. I just want you."

He chuckled before wheezing again. "I'm dying, Evie."

"No! Don't say that." I leaned forward so I could look into his eyes, and when he managed to open them, the pain in his was reflective of the pain in mine.

"Can't heal… not from these burns."

"Please, Zaqiel, no. I need you."

"You're stronger than you think. You always were without me."

His voice was so quiet now, I wanted to grab and shake him, to scream at him to stay with me. "I'm not, though! I'm not strong without you. I need you. Please, tell me what to do."

"Evie…"

"Zaqiel, *please*. You showed me how to live, showed me there was something worth living for. I don't know how to go on without you."

When he didn't answer, I grabbed his face between my hands, his red and black skin flaking under my touch, and I trembled but didn't let him go. Pressing a kiss to his lips, I lingered even as I shook. When I pulled away, I saw the tears trickling down his face and the trails that they left his skin turning to ash and blowing away in the breeze.

He was disappearing right in front of me, and there was nothing I could do to keep him with me.

When I lifted my hands from his face, his head drooped to his chest. I started screaming his name, knowing that my screams were traveling out the alley and down the street, knowing that screaming wasn't helping but unable to stop. Because the pain I felt in my chest was so raw, so intense, there were no words in the world to describe it.

So, I simply screamed.

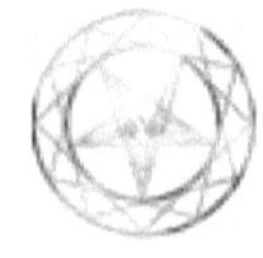

"Shit, it's worse than I thought."

I had screamed until my throat was raw, and I wished I could take every scar on my body and live through it over and over again if only it would take away the pain in my chest. Zaqiel still kneeled in front of me, his chin on his chest. He looked like he was praying, but I couldn't see his chest moving. I kneeled in front of him, resting my hands on his.

I looked up at the voice, my vision blurred from the tears, and rubbed my eyes roughly. "Who are you?" I asked.

"I could smell burning holy oil a mile away."

He strutted toward us from the street, his hands in his pockets and his head tilted as he surveyed Zaqiel. He radiated darkness, and I thought surely, this couldn't be an angel because I could *not* imagine an angel making me tremble under his gaze like that.

When he saw me staring, I swear I saw his eyes flash yellow through the veil of his messy dark hair, and that did nothing to enlighten me as to who or what he was.

"Help," I whispered. "Please help him, please."

The man fell to his knees next to me and lifted Zaqiel's chin between his thumb and finger.

"Zaqiel?" he said.

I didn't know if there was a moan because I wanted there to be one so badly, or if I actually heard the sound of his voice.

"Ah, so you're not quite dead yet. Good stuff."

"What are you doing?" I asked.

He turned to me as his expression darkened.

"Stop touching him, you're accelerating the process."

I yanked my hands away from Zaqiel's still form. "What's happening?"

"He's dying."

I choked back another sob, hearing it said out loud only made it so much harder to deal with. "But you can help him, right? Please."

"I'm going to try."

He placed his hands on Zaqiel's temples and closed his eyes.

I had no idea what was happening, but there was a light around where the stranger's skin met Zaqiel's, and it faded with yellow and white that met somewhere in the middle. Zaqiel's skin almost seemed to glow in the darkness of the night as the vapor was absorbed into his skin through the man's fingertips, and I could follow its pathway as it worked its way through his body.

I wanted to ask who this man was and what he was doing, but something was happening that was beyond my understanding, and I was entranced.

When Zaqiel's skin started to turn ashen and flake faster, I screamed at the stranger to stop, turning to him and grabbing at his leather jacket. He removed one hand from Zaqiel's temple long enough to shove me to the side, and when I went to move again, he hissed at me, displaying sharp teeth and yellow eyes, so I stayed put.

It took only a minute or so before the man dropped his hands to his sides, panting with his chin against his chest, a mirror image of Zaqiel before him. But where Zaqiel's skin had taken on a white glow, the stranger's was yellowed.

When he looked at me, his eyes were definitely yellow with thin black slits for irises. I felt like I should be afraid of him, but I wasn't. The darkness that had been around him when he approached seemed lost now, and he looked weak and vulnerable as he watched me watch him.

I jumped when I heard a moan from Zaqiel and clasped my hand to my mouth as I watched his skin heal. The ash blew away, and beneath was still the burned skin, but the burns seemed to be absorbed with the white glow withdrawing back into him, until the man kneeling before me was the man I knew.

"Zaqiel!" I cried, moving to his side again and taking his cheek in my hand.

"Cade," he whispered.

"Cade?"

I turned to the man kneeled beside me, and he nodded against his chest, raising one hand weakly. "Guilty as charged," he mumbled.

"Cade," I repeated and waited until he rolled his head to the side to look at me out of the corner of his eye. "You saved him. Thank you."

CHAPTER
30

ZAQIEL

Hearing them, Evie's screams as she sat next to me only added to the agony of the burning. Angels feel pain, but the burning was pain from another world. There are only a handful of ways to kill an angel, and unfortunately, the most accessible was also the most painful. There weren't exactly angel blades lying around to be collected by just anyone.

But holy oil, if you knew what it could do, people would get their hands on it.

Who would want to kill an angel?

I had made many misjudgments of people while on Earth, but Lee, he threw me completely. I'd never have picked him for the sort to go away and spend weeks figuring out how to kill me, then go through all of that, frightening all those people simply to get to me.

It made me feel a menace and reminded me of all the things Evie went through that she wouldn't have if I weren't here.

But then again, I had saved her, much as she had saved me.

I felt her kiss on my lips when I was dying, and all I could think was if that was the last sensation I felt on this Earth, then I'm glad it was the most beautiful thing known.

Evie.

But her pain, I felt that to my core. I wanted to reassure her, but it would be a lie.

Because the truth was, I *was* dying.

Covered in burns I couldn't heal from and stripped my life essence away, I had no way to recover from that.

Then he showed up.

Of all the beings to save my life, Cade, a demon who owed me a favor.

He gave me his healing powers, part of his life force. The exertion would've greatly weakened him, and he gave me only enough for my healing powers to kick in. Any more, and it would've killed him.

I hadn't done what I did for Cade so he'd owe me. I hadn't even known who he was, but in one act, I cemented a bond with him that he was insistent he would pay back one day. And I guess today was that day.

Thank God.

Her chin still resting on my chest, Evie hung off my shoulder, gripping me so tight it was as if she didn't want to let me go, which was fine with me. I reached forward and lightly slapped Cade on the knee.

"How did you know?" I mumbled.

"Hey." I could hear the smile in his voice, even though in his weakened state, it couldn't be much more than a lift of the corner of his mouth. "You know me. Cops around, I'm not far away." His tone changed as his face dropped. "I smelled the burning holy oil, and I came running, but I didn't know it was you."

His hand lifted, and for a moment, I thought he was going to take my hand, but that would be out of character for Cade and for almost every demon I knew. Instead, he returned the light slap on the leg I had given him. "Got here just in time," he muttered.

It took a great deal of effort, but I lifted my head, finding that he was already looking at me, his eyes a vivid yellow as he had needed to engage his inner demon to save my life.

"Are you okay?" I asked.

He breathed in heavily before releasing a large sigh. "Yeah, I mean, I will be." When he noticed my frown, he smiled, his sharpened teeth visible. "Don't get all emotional on me. I'll recover."

"Thank you."

This whisper came from Evie. She had rolled her head across my shoulder and was staring at Cade, her arms still wrapped around me, squeezing me next to her. I could feel her tears on my shoulder.

I nodded, then stopped when it made my head throb. "Thank you, Cade. I don't know how I can ever repay you."

Pushing himself to his feet, he chuckled. "You already did, remember? Now we're even."

Evie slung my arm over her shoulder as we made our way back to my apartment, which took considerably longer than it had for us to get to the bar in the first place. We managed to avoid the police who dotted around the streets following the hold-up, thanks to Evie's knowledge of the area. Unable to walk straight out of the alleyway because of the *accident* involving the perpetrator and a car, we had to find an alternate route.

As we reached the apartment, she lowered me onto the bed and sat on the edge staring at me for a long while with a deep frown etched into her forehead.

The corner of my lip lifted as I watched her, my

eyelids drooping. I needed to sleep to heal. "I'm going to be okay, Evie."

"Are you sure?" Her voice was so small, it broke me all over again. I can't imagine how it would feel to think I was going to lose her like that after everything we had been through. That heartache and fear would run deep in her for a while. She'd be watching over me, cautious, scared, careful, worrying every minute the deterioration process would start again, and I'd disappear into the wind. "I just need sleep." I continued, "I'll be okay."

"Okay."

Her tone didn't hold any of the reassurance I had tried to get across. But I was so weak, I couldn't explain any more, not right now. Cade had given me enough life force to heal myself, but it would take time.

As she tucked me in, I whispered, "Am I a prisoner?" I almost smiled with my remaining strength.

The corner of her lip lifted. "No, but you're not healed."

"I can take care of myself."

She laughed then, a soft huff of breath. My words were an echo of hers from what seemed like a lifetime ago.

From when she didn't trust me.

From when I didn't know her.

From before I loved her.

Or maybe I loved her from the moment I first saw her.

"No, you can't," she whispered.

"No." I closed my eyes, ready to succumb to the sleep I needed. "I can't."

CHAPTER
31

EVIE

Possibly the longest week of my life was waiting for Zaqiel to wake.

I tried to do as he had done for me and bring him water, but he wasn't human, and the sleep he was in was unlike anything I had seen. He stayed in bed, legs stretched out, and hands folded neatly over his chest, unmoving but for the steady rise and fall of his chest for almost three full days. He didn't stir when I tried to gently wake him to drink, or move when I gently placed a finger dipped in water and ran it across his lips. So there was nothing I could do but wait and trust that he was going through some healing process beyond my understanding.

He hadn't changed, though. I'd have expected after that long, his lips would be dry and his skin would lose the healthy glow of the living. But he was a preserved being in a state of deep slumber as his body healed.

I was finding it hard to sleep, unable to talk to him and be reassured he was okay. I know I was being selfish, but every time I closed my eyes and allowed myself to rest, the sounds of his supernatural screams as he burned filled my ears and mind, and I would wake in a cold sweat. I'd roll over and place a hand on his chest, taking comfort in the rise and fall, and try to sleep again. Initially, I had slept on the couch, but he didn't seem to know I was here, so I decided I'd rather be near him, even if he couldn't hear or see me.

Heidi came to check on me on the fourth day, just to say hi, unaware of the ordeal Zaqiel had been through. She took one look at me and came back half an hour later with some groceries and insisted on washing my hair over the sink and giving it a long-overdue cut since it was apparently clear I wasn't looking after myself. She took several inches off the length, and while it made me feel naked and exposed, it needed it.

I hoped Zaqiel liked it when he woke.

I told her he had been injured while taking down the man who had held up the bar and was resting. It wasn't a lie, and even so, I was completely comfortable giving her that version of the truth. The full truth of who and what he was wasn't mine to share.

But mine to keep.

Clive didn't know anyone who was looking for waitresses, but I had managed to get a few hours a week at a café a few blocks away that mostly served lunches to the hungry tradesmen who worked in the industrial areas nearby. It wasn't much, but it was something.

People openly staring at my scars wasn't new to me, but at the café it seemed more of a morbid curiosity than anything else, so I didn't mind so much. I wasn't there to care what they thought of me anyway. I'd had only two shifts, and after both, I'd race home and to the bedroom, hoping to find Zaqiel awake. But so far, nothing.

I didn't want to admit to myself I was starting to lose hope he'd ever wake.

He had told me he would be okay, and he wouldn't lie to me. So I had to trust and have blind faith he'd be okay.

But it was hard.

On the seventh day, I woke from an uneasy sleep and rolled over, placing my palm on his chest and feeling his steady breathing for a while.

"I hope you didn't take advantage of me."

I scrambled into an upright position, my feet tangling in the sheets, and I had to fight with them a few seconds before I was able to sit up and cup his face, staring at him. His eyes were still closed, but his lips were curved into that almost smile.

"Zaqiel?"

When he opened his eyes, I was again lost in the blue of them. It was like being refreshed and reborn, seeing those eyes again, but without the pain and worry.

Without the flames licking at his chest and neck.

"Evie," he whispered. "You're a sight for sore eyes."

"I see your rest didn't take away how cheesy you are."

He smiled, and before he was able to respond, I pressed my lips to his, aware I was crying and trying to keep my shoulders from shaking. But he knew. Of course, he did. He could feel my pain as acutely as if it were his own. So he wrapped his arms around me, crushing me against his torso while I buried my face in the crook of his neck. I felt him inhale deeply as my hair fluttered around his face. He grumbled and shifted his weight, pulling me so I was lying on top of him and pressed me against his body again.

I guess he didn't want to let me go either.

I flushed with the thought. So this was what it

was like to be needed, to be loved.

I never wanted to be without it again.

Without him.

"You scared me," I whispered against his skin.

"I'm sorry."

"Don't be. I'm just thankful I have you back."

His arms tightened around me, almost knocking the breath from me. I squirmed until he relinquished his grip and pressed my lips against his again. This time he kissed me back, slowly at first, moving his lips against mine. Before his tongue snaked into my mouth, strong and dominant, taking what he wanted, I broke away long enough to take a breath and say his name. Then his fingers curled into my hair and pulled my mouth back against his.

"You need to rest." I gasped, our lips so close they were almost touching.

He kissed his way along my cheek, my chin, flicking his tongue over my earlobe and making me groan. "I'm done resting."

I nodded as I took his mouth again, and his hand wandered down my body, grabbing my ass and pulling my hips against his. He was hard against my thigh, and I felt a warm rush between my legs at the thought of having him again. It had been much too long, and I never wanted to have to go that long again without him touching me, kissing me, being inside me.

I started grinding my hips against him, desperate for the friction.

He chuckled. "Now who's eager?"

I giggled and grabbed at the short hair on his head, retaking his mouth. He grabbed my ass with both hands, moving me against him, using his erection to stimulate me through the sheets and my clothes.

Too many layers.

When I tried to climb off him to get undressed, he growled at me, low and deep and menacing enough for me to stop trying to move. I was about to protest when he flipped me over, kicking the sheet out from around his feet and removing his pants before crawling on top of me, growling again as my legs fell open, welcoming him.

He was losing control. I could feel it as he tugged my t-shirt off harder than necessary and snarling when it tangled in my arms. The smile on his face was deadly as he left the material tangled around my hands, holding them above my head against the pillows. With his other hand, he fought my underwear down my legs, leaving them dangling off one foot and shoving my legs open again.

When he lay back on top of me, I moaned at the feel of his hardness against my inner thighs. Using his hand, he guided the head against my folds, moaning at how wet I already was. Ready for him, waiting for him.

"Have you needed me, Evie?" he whispered against my ear, the feel of his words against my skin making me shudder. He chuckled, low and deep as I simply whimpered and lifted my hips to him. "Tell me." His voice was drunk with the pleasure flowing over me, the anticipation, the desire that surrounded us both and blocked out the outside world. "Tell me you need me."

"I need you, Zaqiel," I whispered, practically panting as I lifted my hips to him again, whimpering as he moved his erection away from my wetness. He'd make me wait, make me beg if he had to. "I love you."

He groaned as he penetrated me, sliding inside in one smooth motion that left my mouth hanging open as I was stretched to accommodate him. When he started moving within me, the pleasure was almost too much. Everything that had happened recently evaporated, and I could feel nothing but him inside me and out. He was everything to me, and I struggled against the fabric that held my hands down as he increased his pace. But he didn't let me go, and that almost smile adorned his lips again as he watched me squirm underneath him, an intense blend of pleasure and frustration at not being able to touch him.

Each time he thrust, it would stretch me anew, not slowing down or allowing me to get used to the intrusion but forcing my body to accommodate him until I was almost screaming with the pleasure of him.

Dropping himself on top of me, he nipped and licked at my neck and shoulder as he trailed a hand down my body, finding my clit with his fingers and working it in small, tight circles. His movements were in sync, and he was in sync with me as he drew me closer to my climax.

When I came around him, my walls clenched around his length. He groaned and pushed through the resistance before building up the pace of his thrusting. He still had my hands pinned above my head, making me take him. I was desperate to wrap my arms around his body and drag my nails down his back. But this was about him claiming me as much as I wanted to submit to him, to fully allow myself to be cared for, and to be loved and needed. So, I opened my legs wider to him, taking everything he had to give.

"Did you mean it?" He panted, and I watched his eyes as they searched mine.

I couldn't think straight. "What?"

"When you said you loved me?"

"Of course, I did." I panted. "I love you."

With a roar that bordered on that supernatural scream, he came inside me, thrusting against me hard, so he was fully buried inside me. I screamed as his wings unfurled in the moment, opening to their full glory and knocking against the light shade on the ceiling before they folded around us both, cocooning us from the world as he collapsed on top of me.

We stayed like that for a while, Zaqiel rocking his hips slowly against mine, still hard as he moved inside me. His wings covered us both like a protective dome. It was a bit surreal, watching the wall of feathers that blocked the room from my vision move and shift with his breathing, knowing they were a part of him. I wasn't afraid of him and had no reason to be. But I was in awe of the beauty of him and all that he was.

How could I not love him?

He had shown me there was good in this world, and he had *been* the good in this world for me and many others. While I now had something to lose, I also had so much to live for, something I had lacked before.

And I don't think I could ever repay him for that.

"You bring out the best in me," I whispered, kissing at his shoulder. His hand had clenched around the t-shirt tangled around my hands when he came, and I was still unable to move my arms.

He chuckled. "I guess you bring out the naughty in me."

I was about to ask what he meant when he rutted against me, hitting the sensitive walls of my pussy as he went deep again. I thought he was going to go again when he slowly pulled out of me, folding his wings away carefully before rolling onto his back and pulling me next to him after I discarded the t-shirt from around my wrists.

His breathing slowed after a while, and I sighed against his chest as he tightened his arm's grip around me. He started tracing his fingers along my back in slow, deliberate lines.

He had memorized every line of me.

But it was still difficult.

"Must you do that?" I whispered. He was tracing my scars again.

"I like the scars."

I almost sobbed but managed to hold it back, burying my face against his side instead and mumbling, "Why?"

He sighed. "I hate that you were hurt the way you were. I also hate everything you had to go through and the reason you have the scars. I hate that you suffered up until the day I found you and beyond. I hate all of that." He took a breath and sighed again. I waited for the bit that was going to make me feel better about this tapestry of pain that marred my body. "But now, they're a reminder of your strength and a show of everything you can endure, and come out the other end, stronger than before."

He rolled his head to look at me, and I forced myself to meet his eyes. He used a thumb to wipe away a stray tear that had fallen down my cheek, and he smiled. Really smiled.

"Evie, to me, you're the absolute best of humanity, and I love you too."

EPILOGUE

ZAQIEL

A few months was needed, and it was longer than I wanted to wait, but it was necessary. Too soon and the link between what Paul did to Evie and his death would've been much too apparent. Besides, I had done my research, and the man was working his way toward being a state politician. I had to get to him now before he became untouchable.

I was doing the world a favor anyway. He wasn't the sort of person who should be in any position of power. Frankly, with the money he had now, was already too much.

Evie didn't ask where I was going, and I didn't tell.

Technically, I tried to tell myself, this wasn't lying to her. I'd tell her what I had done, the role I had to play *after* it was done. Only after she had seen it on the news.

All these thoughts and plans, but there was one big problem.

Angels couldn't kill humans.

Sure, we were more than capable of it, physically they were no threat to us, but there'd be no tolerance for that sort of thing from the Silver City. There were rules that had to be abided by, and murder would be a one-way ticket to being one of the fallen.

Rule number one—no killing humans. Pretty straightforward.

But there were ways around these things.

My siblings weren't stupid, and it wouldn't take much to figure out what I had done. But they had been on Earth long enough now to see the darkness that was around and to know sometimes it was a choice of the lesser of two evils.

At least, I hoped they viewed it this way.

But if this meant I was stripped of my wings, I could handle that, knowing my last act was to rid the Earth of a man who didn't deserve the miracle of life that had been granted to him. I'd live out the rest of my days, mortal, with Evie. I had come to peace with that.

I hadn't called ahead and simply landed on the balcony of the penthouse apartment, pushing the handle so hard the lock snapped, and I was granted access into the spacious dwelling.

Frank was busy fucking somebody.

"Oh, for God's sake, Frank," I said, turning my back as I folded up my wings. His slacks were pooled around his ankles, standing in the middle of the apartment with a woman balanced on his forearms. Thrusting up into her, she clutched onto his shoulders, her skirt yanked up over her waist and shirt ripped open, one heel on the floor nearby and the other dangling from her toes.

"Your fault for not knocking, angel boy." He panted over the slapping sound of their bodies meeting.

Trust him not to stop.

"Frank," the woman whispered between moans. "Who is that?"

"Nobody. Don't worry about it, pet."

"I'll be outside," I muttered as the distinct sound of kissing joined the moans as they continued. Pulling the door closed behind me, I sat on one of the lounge chairs on the balcony, looking out over the lights of the city. From up here, it was hard to imagine all the things that were going on at the other end of this vast cityscape. The sound of traffic was barely audible from this high up, even for me, and the breeze held a pleasant chill. I could see why the demons sought out this sort of living space, so far removed from where they came from.

Angels came from luxury and divinity in our homes and came to Earth to help those who needed it, having to rapidly adapt to the drastic change between environments. But demons didn't have such noble causes for leaving their home.

Still, they weren't all bad.

Not entirely.

Forty minutes later, I heard the door open. Frank paused when he looked at the lock and tossed me a look of distaste. He had pulled his pants back up but was still shirtless and had lost the shoes and socks. His body glistened with sweat, and from the smell of it, other bodily fluids. As he sat next to me, he handed me a glass of whiskey, which I accepted, staring out at the view again.

"Another one of your conquests, I'm guessing," I said. When he growled at me, I glanced at him, my eyebrows shooting up as he ran a hand through his dark hair, longer than when I last saw him. I sniffed the air, tuning my senses into him, and his snarl deepened. "You bonded with her." It wasn't a question, but he nodded anyway. "Wow, congratulations."

"Thanks," he said gruffly, taking a sip of his drink. "What are you doing here, Zaqiel?"

"I have a favor to ask."

"Oh?" I could hear the smirk in his voice without having to face him.

"I need you to kill someone."

He barked with laughter before taking another drink. "Taste the whiskey, Zaqiel."

I did. It was smooth. Expensive.

"Did you hear what I said?"

He chuckled again. "Of course, I did. But no can do, we have rules, too, you know."

"Since when has that stopped you?"

He threw me a sideways look. "I've got something to lose now," he said.

Following his gaze, I looked over my shoulder at the woman walking across the apartment. She gracefully sat on the couch, folding her feet under her, and when she saw Frank looking, she beamed at him. I could almost feel the warmth from Frank as he smiled back in a way I had never seen him do before.

My God, he really loved her.

"It's funny how it happens, isn't it?" I asked.

"What?"

"How it takes only one human to make you see them all differently."

Frank's lip twitched. "I'll stick to my one." Frank glanced at me and barked out a laugh. "Look at you, *smiling* away. You finally figured out how to smile."

"I could always smile. I just never did for *you.*"

"Only for her, huh?"

I didn't answer, grinning into my drink.

Absentmindedly, I swirled the ice cubes in my glass in the silence that followed before finally sighing. "I don't know what to do."

Frank turned back and sunk in his chair. "Why

don't you tell me about it?"

I did. I told him the entire story. Who this man was I wanted dead and why. Frank stayed silent throughout the tale, not taking his eyes from the view in front of us. Every now and then, he'd smirk, and I figured he was judging me, but I no longer cared. Years ago, someone had told me one day I would feel as he did and that I would understand the desire to want to kill a human. At the time, I didn't believe him, but I understood now.

Guess I owed him an apology now.

"The woman in the alleyway." Frank lifted an eyebrow.

"Yes."

"You said you had her. I didn't realize you meant you *had* her."

"Frank." My tone was a warning, and he chuckled again. I wasn't here to listen to his snide comments.

He didn't speak again for a few minutes. Occasionally, he'd rub his chin or run a hand over his face as though he was working his way through possibilities. I hoped he was trying to figure out how to help me. He had no reason to really, but I knew that Frank would know—if an angel wanted someone dead, there was a *very* good reason for it.

I tolerated the silence as long as I could, and just when I thought I was about to break, he spoke.

"I might be able to help us both," he mumbled.

"How?"

Standing abruptly, Frank smiled that award-winning smile at me, the one that adorned magazines and brochures for his company. "The less you know, the better, angel boy."

I downed the last of my whiskey and handed him the empty glass. "Do you need anything from me?"

Frank was grinning now, and it made me feel as though I didn't want to ask what his plan was. He shook his head, never losing the sneer. "No, I got this."

"Frank—"

"Don't ask questions you don't want the answers to, Zaqiel."

I opened my mouth to respond but instead simply nodded.

He was right.

Punching me on the upper arm, I grunted as he moved to go back inside. "You owe me a new lock, asshole. You didn't have to break the door."

"Bill me," I said.

He was still smirking when I took off into the night.

Paul Gilbert's obituary was on the evening news

287

when I was sitting with Evie on the couch. What a loss to society he was, they said. The man who was so generous in his community, a breath of fresh air who was about to break into politics, a hero among men.

All of it lies.

I felt a pang of guilt when an image of his grieving wife flashed on the screen, but my guilt was short-lived. How could I be sure he didn't treat her as he did other women behind closed doors? I couldn't.

I didn't have to be sure. I knew enough of what he *did* do. All the other things he *might* have done, well, that was for someone higher than me to sort out.

I had expected retribution for my actions and to wake up one morning to find I no longer had my wings, only the long deep scars etched into my back where they used to be, a reminder of what I had been and would never be again. But as each day passed since I saw Frank, nothing changed, and I felt no different. I was starting to suspect he hadn't managed to pull it off until I saw the paper while out and about earlier in the day.

Watching Evie out of the corner of my eye, I was slightly concerned at the blank expression that stayed stubbornly on her face while she took in the news. She didn't move, and I wondered if she already suspected my involvement.

Was it wrong of me? Of course.

Do I regret it? Not one damn bit.

I asked my brothers and sisters if they knew anything about it, and they didn't ask why I wanted to know. They said a demon had done it, and I had a surge of dread in my gut, a rippling mass of guilt that threatened to consume me from the inside out. If Frank had been sent back to Hell and had been separated from his bonded partner because of me... that's collateral damage I couldn't accept, and I'd have to come forward.

But no, the name this demon went by on Earth was Peter.

A slimy character. Apparently, he mooched off Frank with constant threats of exposure, and Frank relinquished enough to keep him satiated so he wouldn't cause too much trouble. Then Peter would take the money and splurge and binge for a few months, not caring about the trail of destruction he left in his wake and quite happy to leave it for angels to clean up.

Yes, I was familiar with this demon.

Whether Frank had framed him or somehow convinced him to actually take the kill, I wasn't sure.

Perhaps it was best I didn't know.

Did some demons deserve to be in Hell more than others? Yeah, they did. Much like some humans deserved to be right there with them.

Evie was looking at me now, a cautious sideways glance. I turned my head until I was facing her fully, and she mirrored my movement. Neither of us said a word. I knew what her question was, and I think she knew the answer. I tilted my chin up slightly as if to say *yes, it was me, is that a problem?*

Her eyes darted between mine, and a frown shifted and disappeared across her face several times as she processed the feelings. I knew she was remembering the sort of man he was, what he had done to her, and what he had done to countless other women.

I lifted my arm over the back of the couch between us, holding her eye contact.

The tiniest smile curved in the corner of her lips, and she slid across the cushions and tucked herself under my arm, snuggling against my torso as I pulled her against me. She picked up the remote and changed the channel. There was some movie on, but I couldn't tell you what it was. When she started walking her fingers up my thigh, my back stiffened. She was grinning at me, I know she was, but I stayed staring at the television, failing to keep still when she wrapped her fingers around my cock through my pants. I smirked as she started to rub me, my fingers gripping onto her upper arm and my head dropping back against the back of the couch.

It was hard to dwell on what I had done. She had a way of distracting me, of blocking out the outside world and bringing me crashing into the moment. I think there was some strange form of justice in demons and angels working together to save humans from the worst of the worst.

But Evie, she was still everything to me.

No matter what happened or how many people I helped, now I came home to her and only her, and she was building herself a life she could be proud of. She came home to me, and we claimed each other, devoured each other, and were the best of each other.

When she took me in her mouth, I groaned.

Oh yes, I had definitely found heaven on Earth.

The END

Next in the Unearthly Sins Series
Lure of a Demon

ACKNOWLEDGMENTS

My journey as a writer is still going, and I don't think it will ever stop being a journey. Sometimes it's harder than I thought it would be, but no matter what, in those times, Jason is always there for me and for being strong when I'm not, thank you. Also, for being the perfect soundboard for plots. There's something about talking to you that helps me sort out my thoughts in a way that doesn't happen with anyone else. I suspect many of my characters may not have made it to the page as fully formed as they are if it weren't for you.

To my characters, because after a while, they stop becoming beings that I've created and are almost like living, breathing people I know so well, it's almost as though they're real. And in a weird way, I guess they are. Maybe that makes me crazy, but I think it makes me passionate. Or maybe both.

To the people who know more than I about this journey and what it entails, and have always been happy to share their knowledge and help out when I panic over something that turns out to be minor — Chris, Kate, Kaylene, Kimberly.
Chris, you need to change your name to be Kris because then my K-team will be complete.

To my readers, as always, I'm forever grateful to those who love these worlds as much as I do.

And, of course, family and friends, who keep me excited even when it becomes difficult, by sharing the passion with me, and constantly reminding me they're proud. Because sometimes, it can be difficult to keep going, and the support is never forgotten nor taken for granted.
But then I sit down with my laptop, and those words begin to flow, and my characters live, and all is right again.

CONNECT WITH ME ONLINE

ANGELS AND FIRE BOOKS
Find our exciting stories at:
www.angelsandfirebooks.com.au

READER GROUP

Want access to fun, prizes and sneak peeks?
Join my Facebook Reader Group.
https://www.facebook.com/groups/588038442170571

The Angel in Her

NEWSLETTER

Sign up for my Newsletter.
https://www.subscribepage.com/angelsandfirebooks

BOOKBUB

https://www.bookbub.com/authors/stefanie-dawn

GOODREADS

Add my books to your TBR list
on my Goodreads profile.
https://www.goodreads.com/author/
show/21761217.Stefanie_Dawn

AMAZON

https://www.amazon.com/author/stefaniedawn

WEBSITE

http://www.angelsandfirebooks.com.au/

INSTAGRAM

https://www.instagram.com/angelsandfirebooks

EMAIL

info@angelsandfirebooks.com.au

FACEBOOK

https://www.facebook.com/stefaniedawnwriter

THE AUTHOR

Stefanie Dawn has been a writer and creative soul all her life **and** strives to give her readers stories that they can escape into as they become absorbed in the worlds created.

When she isn't writing, Stefanie might be painting, reading, or watching movies. She loves the process of producing films as another form of storytelling. There's also a good chance she will be baking some delicious treats—pretending she won't later regret consuming them—or simply enjoying a cocktail with friends.

Stefanie Dawn lives in South Australia with her ever-supportive partner and a lovable gang of rescue cats.

You can stay up to date with
Stefanie and her books at:
www.angelsandfirebooks.com.au

www.ingramcontent.com/pod-product-compliance
Lightning Source LLC
Chambersburg PA
CBHW051130190726
48290CB00006B/1772